IN THE LAND OF SMALL DRAGON

IN THE LAND OF SMALL DRAGON

A VIETNAMESE FOLKTALE

To the memory of Sister Michael

TOLD BY DANG MANH KHA
TO ANN NOLAN CLARK
ILLUSTRATED BY TONY CHEN

THE VIKING PRESS, NEW YORK

ONE

Man cannot know the whole world,
But can know his own small part.

In the Land of Small Dragon,
In the Year of the Chicken,
In a Village of No-Name,

In the bend of the river,
There were many small houses
Tied together by walkways.
Mulberry and apricot,
Pear tree and flowering vine
Dropped their delicate blossoms
On a carpet of new grass.

In a Village of No-Name
Lived a man and two daughters.
Tấm was the elder daughter;
Her mother died at her birth.

A jewel box of gold and jade
Holds only jewels of great price.

Tấm's face was a golden moon,
Her eyes dark as a storm cloud,
Her feet delicate flowers
Stepping lightly on the wind.
No envy lived in her heart,
Nor bitterness in her tears.

Cám was the younger daughter,
Child of Number Two Wife.

Cám's face was long and ugly,
Scowling and discontented,
Frowning in deep displeasure.
Indolent, slow and idle,
Her heart was filled with hatred
For her beautiful sister.

An evil heart keeps records
On the face of its owner.

The father loved both daughters,
One not more than the other.
He did not permit his heart
To call one name more dearly.

He lived his days in justice,
Standing strong against the wind.

Father had a little land,
A house made of mats and clay,
A grove of mulberry trees
Enclosed by growing bamboo,
A garden and rice paddy,
Two great water buffalo,
A well for drinking water,
And twin fish ponds for the fish.

Cám's mother, Number Two Wife,
Cared only for her own child.
Her mind had only one thought:
What would give pleasure to Cám.

Her heart had only one door
And only Cám could enter.

Number Two Wife was jealous
Of Tấm, the elder daughter,
Who was beautiful and good,
So the mother planned revenge
On the good, beautiful child.

To Cám she gave everything,
But nothing but work to Tấm.

Tấm carried water buckets,
Hanging from her bamboo pole.
Tấm carried forest fagots
To burn in the kitchen fire.
Tấm transplanted young rice plants
From seed bed to rice paddy.
Tấm flailed the rice on a rock,
Then she winnowed and gleaned it.

Tấm's body ached with tiredness,
Her heart was heavy and sad.
She said, "Wise Father, listen!
I am your elder daughter;
Therefore why may I not be
Number One Daughter, also?

"A Number One Daughter works,
But she works with dignity.
If I were your Number One
The honor would ease my pain.
As it is, I am a slave,
Without honor or dignity."

Waiting for wisdom to come,
Father was slow to give answer.
"Both my daughters share my heart.
I cannot choose between them.
One of you must earn the right
To be my Number One child."

A man's worth is what he does,
Not what he says he can do.

"Go, Daughters, to the fish pond;
Take your fish baskets with you.
Fish until night moon-mist comes.
Bring your fish catch back to me.
She who brings a full basket
Is my Number One Daughter.
Your work, not my heart, decides
Your place in your father's house."

Tấm listened to her father
And was quick to obey him.
With her basket, she waded
In the mud of the fish pond.
With quick-moving, graceful hands
She caught the quick-darting fish.

Slowly the long hours went by.
Slowly her fish basket filled.

Cám sat on the high, dry bank
Trying to think of some plan,
Her basket empty of fish,
But her mind full of cunning.
"I, wade in that mud?" she thought.
"There must be some better way."

At last she knew what to do
To be Number One Daughter.

"Tấm," she called, "elder sister,
Our father needs a bright flower,
A flower to gladden his heart.
Get it for him, dear sister."

Tấm, the good, gentle sister,
Set her fish basket aside
And ran into the forest
To pick the night-blooming flowers.

Cám crept to Tấm's fish basket,
Emptied it into her own.
Now her fish basket was full.

Tấm's held only one small fish.
Quickly Cám ran to Father,
Calling, "See my full basket!"

Tấm ran back to the fish pond
With an armload of bright flowers.
"Cám," she called, "what has happened?
What has happened to my fish?"

Slowly Tấm went to Father
Bringing him the flowers and fish.

Father looked at both baskets.
Speaking slowly, he told them,
"The test was a full basket,
Not flowers and one small fish.
Take your fish, Elder Daughter.
It is much too small to eat.
Cám has earned the right to be
Honorable Number One."

TWO

Tấm looked at the little fish.
Her heart was filled with pity
At its loneliness and fright.
"Little fish, dear little fish,
I will put you in the well."

At night Tấm brought her rice bowl,
Sharing her food with the fish—
Talked to the thin fish, saying,
"Little fish, come eat with me"—
Stayed at the well at nighttime
With the stars for company.

The fish grew big and trustful.
It grew fat and not afraid.
It knew Tấm's voice and answered,
Swimming to her outstretched hand.

Cám sat in the dark shadows,
Her heart full of jealousy,
Her mind full of wicked thoughts.
Sweetly she called, "Tấm, sister.
Our father is overtired.
Come sing him a pretty song
That will bring sweet dreams to him."

Quickly Tấm ran to her father,
Singing him a nightbird song.

Cám was hiding near the well,
Watching, waiting and watching.
When she heard Tấm's pretty song
She crept closer to the fish,
Whispering, "Dear little fish,
Come to me! Come eat with me."

The fish came, and greedy Cám
Touched it, caught it and ate it!

Tấm returned. Her fish was gone.
"Little fish, dear little fish,
Come to me! Come eat with me!"
Bitterly she cried for it.

The stars looked down in pity;
The clouds shed teardrops of rain.

THREE

Tấm's tears falling in the well
Made the water rise higher.
And from it rose Nang Tien,
A lovely cloud-dressed fairy.
Her voice was a silver bell
Ringing clear in the moonlight.

"My child, why are you crying?"
"My dear little fish is gone!
He does not come when I call."
"Ask Red Rooster to help you.
His hens will find Little Fish."

Soon the hens came in a line
Sadly bringing the fish bones.

Tấm cried, holding the fish bones.
"Your dear fish will not forget.
Place his bones in a clay pot
Safe beneath your sleeping mat.
Those we love never leave us.
Cherished bones keep love alive."

In her treasured clay pot, Tấm
Made a bed of flower petals
For the bones of Little Fish
And put him away with love.

But she did not forget him;
When the moon was full again,
Tấm, so lonely for her fish,
Dug up the buried clay pot.

Tấm found, instead of fish bones,
A silken dress and two jeweled *hai.**
Her Nang Tien spoke again.

* *hai:* shoes

"Your dear little fish loves you.
Clothe yourself in the garments
His love has given you."

Tấm put on the small jeweled *hai*.
They fit like a velvet skin
Made of moonlight and stardust
And the love of Little Fish.

Tấm heard music in her heart
That sent her small feet dancing,
Flitting like two butterflies,
Skimming like two flying birds,
Dancing by the twin fish ponds,
Dancing in the rice paddy.

But the mud in the rice paddy
Kept one jeweled *hai* for its own.

Night Wind brought the *hai* to Tấm
"What is yours I bring to you."
Water in the well bubbled,
"I will wash your *hai* for you."

Water buffalo came by.
"Dry your *hai* on my sharp horn."
A blackbird flew by singing,
"I know where this *hai* belongs.
In a garden far away
I will take this *hai* for you."

FOUR

What is to be must happen
As day follows after night.

In the Emperor's garden,
Sweet with perfume of roses,
The Emperor's son, the Prince,
Walked alone in the moonlight.

A bird, black against the moon,
Flew along the garden path,
Dropping a star in its flight.
"Look! A star!" exclaimed the Prince.
Carefully he picked it up
And found it was the small jeweled *hai.*

"Only a beautiful maid
Can wear this beautiful *hai.*"
The Prince whispered to his heart,
And his heart answered, "Find her."

In truth, beauty seeks goodness:
What is beautiful is good.

The Prince went to his father:
"A bird dropped this at my feet.
Surely it must come as truth,
Good and fair the maid it fits.
Sire, if it is your pleasure
I would take this maid for wife."

The Great Emperor was pleased
With the wishes of his son.
He called his servants to him,
His drummers and his crier,
Proclaiming a Festival
To find one who owned the *hai.*

In the Village of No-Name
The Emperor's subjects heard—
They heard the Royal Command.
There was praise and rejoicing.
They were pleased the Royal Son
Would wed one of their daughters.

FIVE

Father's house was filled with clothes,
Embroidered *áo-dài** and *hai*
Of heavy silks and rich colors.
Father went outside to sit.

Cám and her mother whispered
Their hopes, their dreams and their plans.

Cám, Number One Daughter, asked,
"Mother, will the Prince choose me?"

Mother said, "Of course he will.
You will be the fairest there!
When you curtsy to the Prince
His heart will go out to you."

Tấm, Daughter Number Two, said,
"May I go with you and Cám?"
Cám's mother answered curtly,
"Yes, if you have done this task:

* *áo-dài:* long robes

Separating rice and husks
From one basket into two."

Tấm knew Cám's mother had mixed
The cleaned rice with rice unhusked.

She looked at the big basket
Full to brim with rice and husks.
Separating the cleaned rice
From that of rice unhusked
Would take all harvest moon time,
When the Festival would end.

A cloud passed over the moon.
Whirring wings outsung the wind.
A flock of blackbirds lighted
On the pile of leaves and grain.
Picking the grain from the leaves,
They dropped clean rice at Tấm's feet.

Tấm could almost not believe
That the endless task was done.

Tấm, the elder daughter, said,
"May I go? May I go, too,
Now that all my work is done?"

Cám taunted, "How could you go?
You have nothing fit to wear."

"If I had a dress to wear
Could I go to the Palace?"
"If wishes were dresses, yes,
But wishes are not dresses."
When Mother left she said,
"Our dear Cám is ravishing.
Stay at home, you Number Two!
Cám will be the one to wed."

Tấm dug up the big clay pot
The dress and one *hai* were there—
As soft as misty moon clouds,
Delicate as rose perfume.

Tấm washed her face in the well,
Combed her hair by the fish pond.
She smoothed down the silken dress,
Tied one *hai* unto her belt
And, though her feet were bare,
Hurried, scurried, ran and ran.

She ran to the Festival
In the King's Royal Garden.

At the Palace gates the guards
Bowed before her, very low.

Pretty girls stood in a line
With their mothers standing near;
One by one they tried to fit
A foot into a small, jeweled *hai*.

Cám stood beside her mother,
By the gilded throne-room door.
Her face was dark and angry
Like a brooding monsoon wind.

Cám, wiping her tears away,
Sobbed and whimpered and complained,
"My small foot fits his old shoe—
Everything but my big toe."

Tấm stood shyly by the door
Looking in great wonderment
While trumpeters and drummers
Made music for her entrance.

People looked at gentle Tấm.
Everyone was whispering,
"Oh! She is so beautiful!
She must be a Princess fair
From some distant foreign land."

Then the Prince looked up and saw
A lady walking toward him.

Stepping from his Royal Throne,
He quickly went to meet her,
And taking her hand led her
To His Majesty the King.

What is to be must happen
As day happens after night.

Real beauty mirrors goodness.
What is one is the other.

Kneeling, the Prince placed the *hai*
On Tấm's dainty little foot.
Tấm untied the *hai* she wore
And slid her bare foot in it.

Beauty is not painted on.
It is the spirit showing.

The Prince spoke to his father.
"I would take this maid for wife."
His Royal Highness nodded.
"We will have a Wedding Feast."
All the birds in all the trees
Sang a song of happiness:
"Tấm, the Number Two Daughter,
Is to be Wife Number One."

What is written in the stars
Cannot be changed or altered.

About the Authors

DANG MANH KHA was born in Vietnam, was educated at St. John's University in Minnesota, and served for four years as a teacher in El Paso, Texas. In August 1975 he devoted his time to helping the Vietnamese refugees as Assistant Administrator for the Southeast Asian Resettlement Program. He now lives in Tucson, Arizona.

ANN NOLAN CLARK was born in Las Vegas, New Mexico, and served for many years as a teacher and writer for the Bureau of Indian Affairs, the State Department, and the U.S. Department of Education in Latin America. She has written numerous books about children in different parts of the world, including *In My Mother's House,* a Caldecott Honor Book, and *The Secret of the Andes,* set in Peru, which won the Newbery Medal. In 1963 Mrs. Clark received the Regina Medal from the Catholic Library Association for "continued distinguished contributions to literature for children." Mrs. Clark's most recent book was *To Stand Against the Wind,* a story about a young Vietnamese boy's recollections of his past. She lives near Tucson, Arizona.

About the Artist

TONY CHEN is the award-winning illustrator of more than twenty-six children's books. Born in the West Indies, he came to New York in 1949 and was graduated with honors from Pratt Institute, Brooklyn. He has had seven one-man shows in New York and has received awards and citations of merit from the Society of Illustrators, *Art Direction* magazine, and The Educational Press Association. Mr. Chen lives with his family in New York City.

About this book

The color art for *In the Land of Small Dragon* was prepared in watercolors and pen and ink. The art was then camera separated and printed in four colors. The black-and-white artwork was drawn in pen and ink with ink washes, then shot as a halftone and printed in black.

The text type is 14-point Linotype Granjon, and the display type is Typositor Carolus Roman.

First Edition

First published in 1979 by The Viking Press, 625 Madison Avenue, New York, N.Y. 10022
Published simultaneously in Canada by Penguin Books Canada Limited
Printed in U.S.A.
1 2 3 4 5 83 82 81 80 79

Library of Congress Cataloging in Publication Data
Clark, Ann Nolan. In the Land of Small Dragon.
Summary: In the Land of Small Dragon, a dutiful daughter,
mistreated by her stepmother, is rewarded by her fairy godmother.
[1. Fairy tales. 2. Folklore—Vietnam]
I. Clark, Ann Nolan. II. Chen, Tony. III. Title.
PZ8.K52In 398.2'1'09597[E] 78-26233 ISBN 0-670-39697-4

DD688283

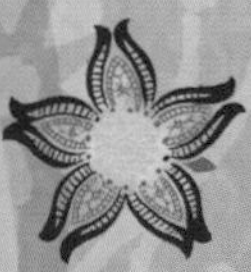

Praise for *SHE*

"*SHE* is a beautiful tribute and, above all, a celebration of the incredible power of women. I was moved and inspired by this gorgeously illustrated book of qualities. In today's busy world, it is good to read reminders of what those who came before us have done to make this a better world. The voices of these remarkable women sing off the page. Here's to great women!"

—June Cotner,
author of *Graces* and *Garden Blessings*

"I am quite taken with this beautiful book. *SHE* is a stunning capture of who we are as women sprinkled with simple ideas to grow deeper into our capacities. Intrigued by every aspect of the feminine, I 'found myself' on every page! *SHE* is a gift I will bestow on all my friends!"

—Lisa Venable,
author of *Messages from Love*

"Mary Anne has the ability to communicate true wisdom, practical motivation, and fun in a simple yet profound way. This is her true genius."

—Connie Fails

"Liz Kalloch's work is a reflection of her soul—extraordinarily beautiful. She captures details and wonder that others miss, plus she does it with a grace that makes her work even more special."

—Jolie Guillebeau,
painter and storyteller

"Mary Anne Radmacher exudes and lives her message every day. She is one of the most authentic, inspiring, and alive women I know. Her art and writing are extensions of her glowing spirit, and a direct transmission."

—Jennifer Louden,
author of *The Life Organizer* and *The Woman's Comfort Book*

"Mary Anne Radmacher is one-of-a-kind. Her ability to convey ideas in a very engaging way is exceptional, and her passion for life is amazing. She's not only one of my favorite authors, she's also one of my favorite people."

—Mac Anderson,
founder of Successories and CEO of Simple Truths

"Mary Anne and Liz have created an original and beautiful book for women that will become a true classic.... Experience wonderment as you read through the gifts of women that they highlight on these lovely pages. *SHE* is a ticket to self-love, acceptance, and fulfillment for women—an engaging antidote to fear and lack of confidence...like a glorious massage for the soul."

—Gail McMeekin,
author of *The 12 Secrets of Highly Creative Women*

"Liz has a way of moving through the world with an open heart that makes her a joy to be around. She is a kindred spirit who deeply listens and teaches me to trust my creative intuition...she wants to understand who you are and enhance the stories you are sharing with her creative toolbox full of colors, patterns, and wisdom."

—Liz Lamoreux,
author of *Inner Excavation*

"'My presence is proof of my value and that is always enough,' writes Mary Anne Radmacher in the preface of *SHE*; and this beautiful book, with its whimsical art and lyrical prose, is more than enough. In it, authors Radmacher and Kalloch remind us clearly and beautifully that our magnificence is in our kindness, creativity, and intelligence. It is in our willingness to live openly. *SHE* is just the book that can inspire women everywhere to tap into that, their true nature."

—Polly Campbell,
author of *Imperfect Spirituality*

"Not only are Liz Kalloch's artful constructions beautiful, she is a gorgeous person inside and out. I believe her calm and gentle spirit and her patient attention to detail most certainly have an influence on her work. When Liz looks out at the world, I imagine her view is like a kaleidoscope, an ever-changing landscape of color and pattern and symmetry—an ornamental template that influences her work and her life."

—Amy Williamson,
owner and teacher at Brave Girls Art

"Mary Anne Radmacher generously brings her stories and experiences to life on the page. Her words are simple and easy to grasp, woven together in an easy to understand way."

—Beth Miller,
author of *The Woman's Book of Resilience*

"Few authors are as original, insightful, and multi-talented as Mary Anne Radmacher. In *SHE*, her words sing and Liz Kalloch's art soars...lifting your heart, mind, and soul simultaneously. Beautiful, just beautiful!"

—BJ Gallagher,
author of *It's Never Too Late to Be What You Might Have Been*

"Liz has that magical combination of being highly creative and deeply knowledgeable. She is over and beyond capable of any design project you engage her in. And she is one of these passionate people who design late at night on and off the computer in equal measure. She's the real thing. She executes professionally and creatively and is simply a delight to work with."

—Niya Sisk,
Creative Director at Ritual Labs

"Liz Kalloch is so much more than a designer to me. Her collaboration is more expansive than mock-ups or layouts—she catches my dreams and helps me imagine and shape them into reality. Her expertise in publishing, packaging, and product development—on top of her gifted eye and deep intuition—converge, and I have five advisers in one."

—Jen Lee,
storyteller and filmmaker at Jen Lee Productions

"Mary Anne is simply one of the most eclectic, creative, and inspiring people I am fortunate to know. She is every person's greatest mirror for finding one's own gifts, talents, and resources. I cannot help but smile just thinking of her..."

—Dr. Craig Weiner, DC

SHE

SHE

A celebration of Greatness in Every Woman

By Mary Anne Radmacher
and Liz Kalloch
Foreword by Jane Kirkpatrick

viva
EDITIONS

S

Published in the United States by Viva Editions,
an imprint of Cleis Press, Inc., 2246 Sixth Street, Berkeley, California 94710.

Printed in China.
Primary Art: Liz Kalloch
Writing: Mary Anne Radmacher
Book Design: Frank Wiedemann
First Edition.
10 9 8 7 6 5 4 3 2 1

Hardcover ISBN: 978-1-936740-72-7
E-book ISBN: 978-1-936740-74-1

Table of contents

Foreword

Toward the end of my first reading of *SHE*, when I read Kim Hamilton's contribution in *She is a model of balance*, an unexpected prick pushed against my nose; tears pooled in my eyes; and I wept. I'd been reading as a writer who celebrates historical women and asked by author/artist Mary Anne Radmacher to prepare a foreword. As a writer, I hoped to capture the essence of this work to share with others. I responded instead as a reader, swept away by the steady, delicate dance of art and story winging its way directly to my soul.

Through visually enriching images, carefully selected bits of wisdom, and singular words, the contributors to *SHE* take readers aloft, cherishing even the parts of a woman's life we've forgotten are within us or perhaps never celebrated before: *Intrepid traveler. Exquisite aesthetic. Purposeful risk taker. SHE* is twenty-five threads of a woman's being woven into sensory stories easily accessed whether seeking insight or wishing for that quiet moment of understanding. The very design of the pages reminds the reader of precious books of old whose lithographs we wish were framed to grace our walls as well as illustrate our books.

Inspirational books are meant to help us breathe in new dreams, give us confidence to be at one with courage. *SHE* does this and more. With its particular brushstrokes of gorgeous designs and the poetic selection of words, *SHE* fills the spirit with memories of women long past, washes our contemporary souls with the infusion of strong, beautiful women present, and melts frozen seas within us that we might sail with confidence into new vistas.

When my older sister was very ill, she noted that when in a wilderness place, it's hard to concentrate long enough to read an entire book to help one through. Small bits of wisdom, art, and story became the balm that nurtured her last days. *SHE*, while meant to celebrate the female spirit, is also a book of healing offered on a platter of visual beauty. It can be entered anywhere, at any page and savored for a moment or a month of struggle through uncertainty; or when seeking words to celebrate the women in our lives. It is a book that harnesses everything.

The word *celebrate* arrives from the Latin *celebrāre*, meaning "to fill up" and it suggests that we do so "frequently." *SHE* is a unique, celebrating book that I will read often and will gift to my women friends that they might feel known, cherished and loved just as *SHE* has gifted me.

Jane Kirkpatrick

INTRODUCTION

Consider the possibility of soaring.

What is often perceived as failure is better understood as practice.

A bird is not born able to fly but rather a bird IS born equipped to fly.

The moment when consistent attempts/practice intersects with appropriate development and right timing, that is the moment when a bird can fly. The potential for flight is within them, from the beginning. It just takes time.

You are also equipped to fly. You have everything it takes to soar.

All those attempts that look like failures? They are attempts, exercise, practice. Each effort defines a woman's capacity, her unique style. At that ideal intersection when effort and equipment work wonderfully together with personal desire and vision, it will be no surprise, at all, that YOU SOAR, you will soar and you can keep on soaring.

Too many people expect perfection or, at least, practically perfect, the first time they try something. Without that immediate satisfaction of quick mastery, they assess that they can't do it.
"I'm no good at this."
"I haven't the native talent for this."
"I'm just not ________(artistic, creative, athletic, witty, funny)."

That something brings you pleasure is reason enough to pursue it. It does not require immediate mastery or even that you eventually do it "perfectly."

Could the ancient wisdom of fall seven times get up eight sound like:
Leap. Fall, Get up. Jump. Fall. Get up. Skip a little. Fall. Get up?
Rather than considering those falls failures, consider them training for soaring. Brain specialists assert that the brain has to pave new pathways while embracing a new skill, pursuit, idea, vision. Laying down a new road takes time whether it's a county road crew laying asphalt or you discovering ways of thinking or behaving.

The key word is discovering. Uncovering. Unfolding. There are extraordinary capacities held within you, some of which you only have a whisper of an idea. You don't have to go get them, learn them, apply them. You already have what you need within you. Here you will connect with the wisdom of dozens of amazing women, just like you. Through phrase, shared experience, and stories, you will begin to see how these women harnessed their personal capacity and natural strengths to make significant contributions to their own lives and the lives of their circle.

SHE (She Harnesses Everything)—is a Celebration of Greatness in Every Woman. It is your personal Book of Hours. Allow it to inspire you, call you to courageous ways of seeing how lovely, how awesome, how amazing you truly are.

Mary Anne Radmacher and Liz Kalloch

PREFACE

This is a celebration of all the things that a woman is in a single day. More than WHAT she does, WHO she is. A woman's day cannot be characterized in a single expression. The day of a SHE is as diverse as the woman herself. Images of vintage women are featured here. They are our greatness, our collective history. These portraits belong to every women. They are the mothers, the sisters, the friends that collaborated for equal voice, the right to vote, the opportunity to be and serve in community as partners toward creating a better world.

The women who populate my circle of friends and who lead my list of s/heroes seize everything in life as opportunity. Yes,

She
Harnesses
Everything.

Some days I picture that as preparing a horse for a cantering trot and other days it's as if she is fitting reins on the muzzle of the sea.

SHE recognizes that there is possibility for good in all things—as basic as the chance to learn a path to never travel again.

SHE is as comfortable in the silence of the early dawn as she is in the populated center of attention.

SHE is universal truth found in the Divine Feminine (yes, that means men can demonstrate SHE attributes, too). SHE is found in the faces and qualities and life experiences of those you admire, many of whom are women who stand or sit in the circles of your friendships.

SHE is a companion to celebrate and invite the many strengths, qualities and joys that punctuate the stories of your life. SHE is the reflection you catch of yourself, early in your day in the mirror, by a happenstance glance reflecting your quick gait in the glass of a storefront...

SHE is the voice of wisdom that resides within you. Go ahead and ask her.

She knows to embrace the tears and then turn around to welcome triumph, how to be grounded in grief and allow that deep understanding of loss to create a pathway to gratitude. Seeing that sorrow is a stepping off point for soaring.

The wisdom of SHE who dwells within you knows that procrastination may seem like a shortcoming but can be leveraged as a tool used to complete things. Yes, shortcomings turn into shortcuts and produce outcomes different than anyone might guess.

Alone, or in the company of her friends, in the way, or on the way, she can be silent, content with her knowing or can speak her truth, with no apology.

SHE rarely has to wait anywhere, because she always has something to create, contemplate or consider.

Inconvenience is turned to discovery and, as a matter of habit, when she travels she leaves all her shoulds and oughts at home.

SHE harnesses every aspect of her life to the greatest advantage of her heart, her purpose and her intention. She takes the time to invest in her own health, wellness and contentment. And it is to all these aspects of the diverse, dynamic and divine SHE that this book is dedicated and addressed.

Mary Anne Radmacher and Liz Kalloch

I do good in the world with my money. I contribute to those in need, give my gifts to inspire others to give generously. I service the debts of my past and meet my obligations with my resources. I am not defined by my money.

I brighten the world with things. My home environment is eclectic and is populated by meaningful objects. I create things that other people use to decorate and give as gifts. I am not defined by things. I am not defined by what I create.

I move. Quickly and purposefully. I watch my minutes like a dog protecting its last bone. I always have minutes to lavish on my friends. I am not defined by how I spend my time. I am not defined by my physical activity.

I am not where I've been, how I dress, what I look like. I am not whom I know, the influence I wield or how much I donate, contribute or volunteer. I am not what I fear.

My value is measured by the enlivening breath of spirit that animates me. I am defined by my lungs expanding with the very breath of God.

I see because I have been seen by the ultimate love. I am defined by the print made by my feet - that declares my presence on this earth defines me. My presence is proof of my value and that is always enough.

Always.

she dances.
she sings. she takes.
she gives.
she serves. she loves.
she creates. she is fierce.
she dissents. she
enlivens.
she sees. she grows.
she sweats.
she changes.
she learns. she laughs.
she sheds her skin.
she bleeds on
the pages of her days.
she walks through walls.
she lives with
intention.

—mary anne radmacher, 1997

she is full of longing. she overflows with ideas to make the world a better, kinder, more interesting place. she tests and experiments with powerful statements and gracious actions., then she recommends them to others.

she is vulnerable, honest and seeks her own knowing with diligence. she aspires to a well-lived day, not a well-mannered day.

she supposes IMPOSSIBLE can be seen as "I * M * possible." she uses expletives for emphasis without apology. Her kindness exists beyond the rule of others.

she believes in her dreams and does at least one thing toward them each day.

she is willing.

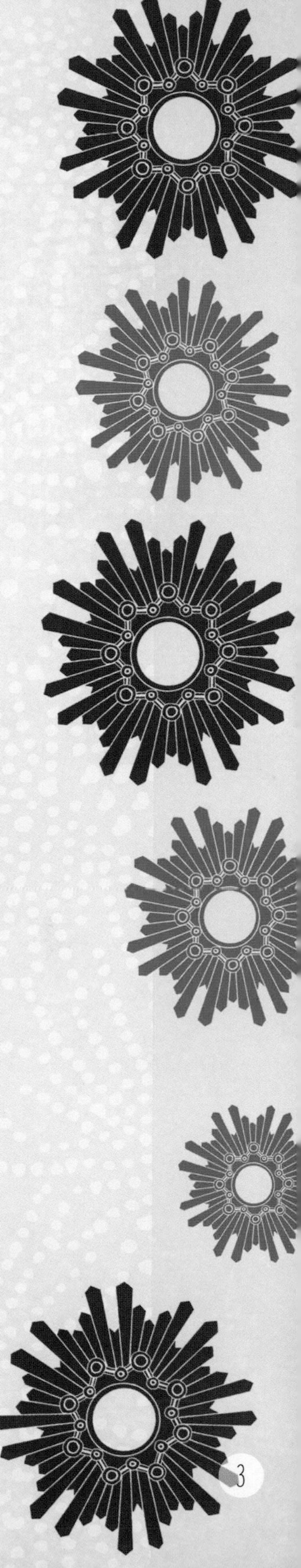

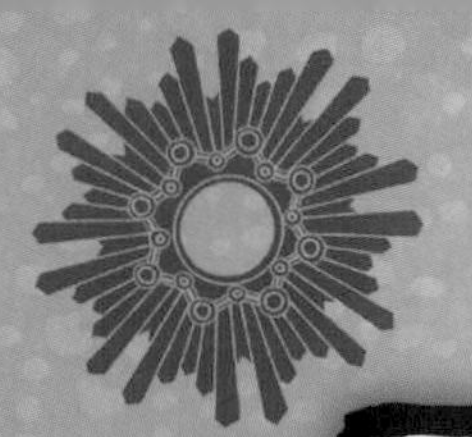

Set up camp on the very edge of your comfort zone, your willingness to step outside of it regularly, will deepen your footpath to courage. It will build sturdy bridges to your bravery. Your willingness to make and play your own rules, clears the water of murk while you dive into the deepest parts of yourself. Your willingness to constantly and consistently choose kindness and love over fear and hate, to NOT let petty drama rule your life, takes more guts and grit than most anything. Take pride in your actions. Feel what you feel, but rise above, dear you. You are exactly where you are supposed to be, you are way beyond enough, your willingness to really and truly BELIEVE that, your willingness to deem yourself worthy of nothing but love will be your compass AND your flashlight to a life of joy.

-Amanda Oaks

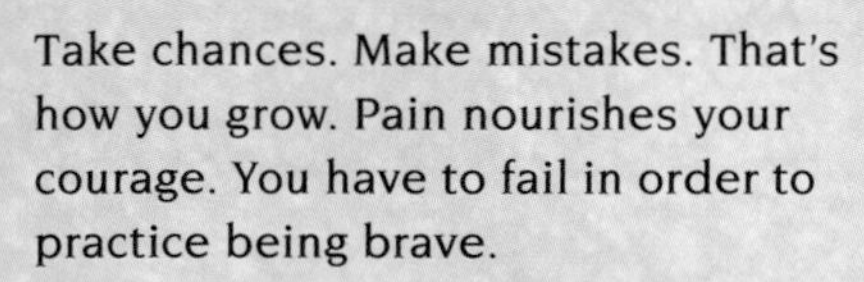

Take chances. Make mistakes. That's how you grow. Pain nourishes your courage. You have to fail in order to practice being brave.

-MARY TYLER MOORE

I have always grown from my problems and challenges, from things that don't work out; that's when I've really learned.

-CAROL BURNETT

You have to have confidence in your ability, and then be tough enough to follow through.

-ROSALYNN CARTER

One cannot and must not try to erase the past merely because it does not fit the present.

-GOLDA MEIR

One never notices what has been done; one can only see what remains to be done.

-MARIE CURIE

Only when we are no longer afraid do we begin to live.

-DOROTHY THOMPSON

Dear Kind One,

Willingness wears many different faces. And not all of them are colored with the first crayons you'd be inclined to pull out of the box. Sometimes willingness says, "No," more readily than "yes." Occasionally it says, "Enough, now," instead of "Here, have more."

Be willing—as best as you can, as often as you can.

Perhaps it strikes you as kind of wimpy to say, "as best you can?" Seriously. That's all you've got, girl? And some days the answer is, "Yep. That's it." Willingness is often better informed upon reflection, upon glancing back. How easily the choices fill in from that backwards glance that did not seem visible at the moment of choice. Willingness has a certain component of faithfulness about it—a devotion to the most kind outcome. Which is essential in that moment of choice when you haven't any idea what the outcome will be.

While many are inclined to consider willingness something one is, I am increasingly convinced that actions and words play into willingness more than I ever used to give them credit. Much open-mindedness occurs in the realm of what I choose NOT to say, and actions that I opt to pass on. Even holding back that immediate, "You've got to be kidding," when I stand in disbelief at some shocking action, is an act of willingness. Seem complex, or somewhat ironic? Well, if willingness was simple and easy then everyone would be it and do it.

And to that reference of irony—the greatest helpfulness can masquerade as an action or attitude that first appears unkind. On the big scale of openness to change that seems counter to intuition...a dear woman once fired me. Yep. Handed me my walking papers. Rather abruptly, I might add. "And I thought she was my friend," I remember thinking that day. Ha. Turns out she was. Firing me was the greatest invitation to being willing she could have served up—I began fuller attention to things that had been struggling under my distracted, part-time attention.

The more I invite myself to be persuadable (by myself and others)—as best as I'm able—the more I'm surprised by all the different outfits willingness wears. The great thing is this—all the variety of costumes that willingness dresses in—they all have some element of possibility attached and each one fits perfectly.

In the spirit of open willingness,

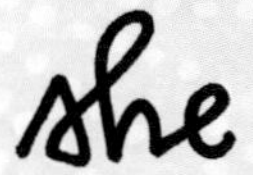

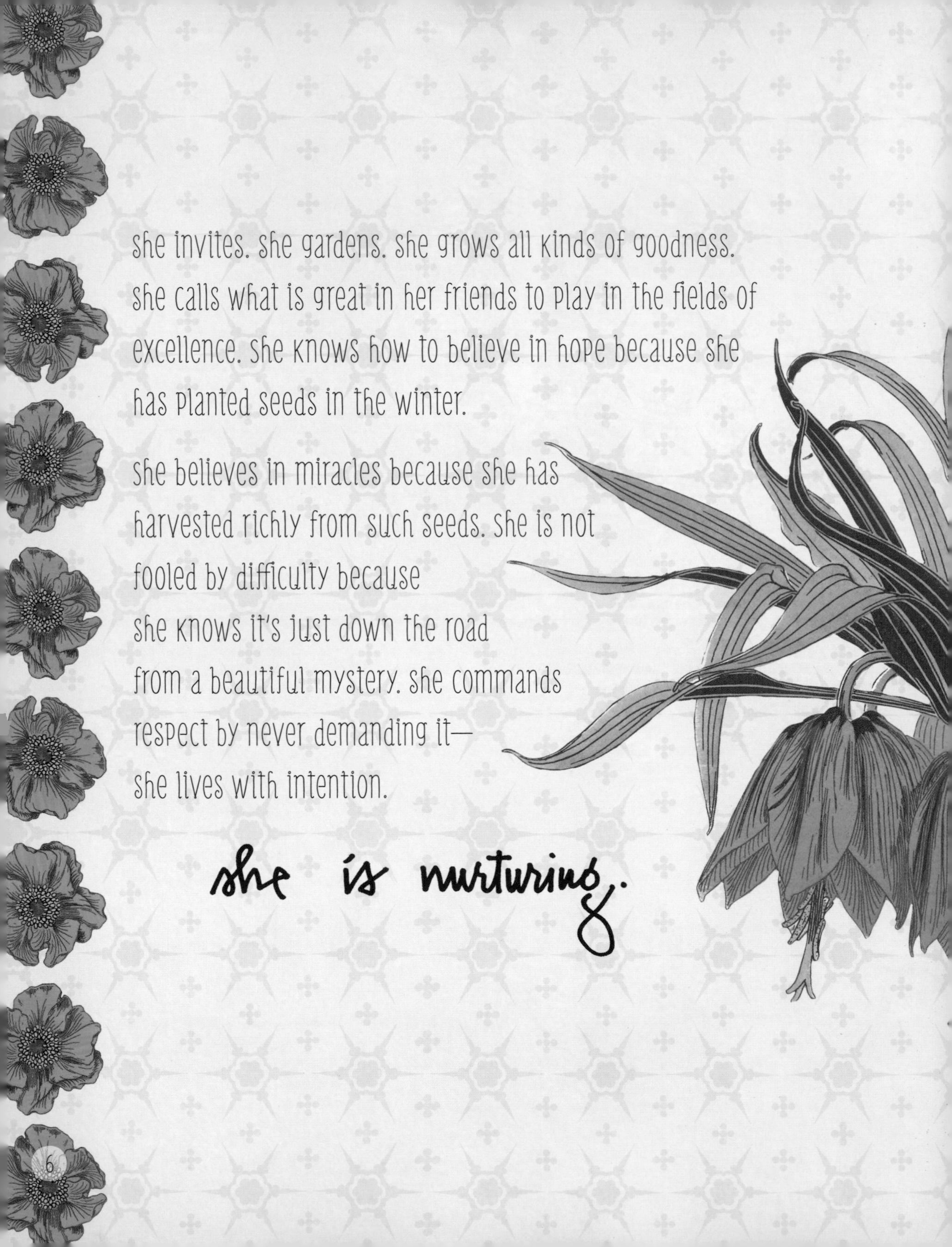

she invites. she gardens. she grows all kinds of goodness. she calls what is great in her friends to play in the fields of excellence. she knows how to believe in hope because she has planted seeds in the winter.

she believes in miracles because she has harvested richly from such seeds. she is not fooled by difficulty because
she knows it's just down the road
from a beautiful mystery. she commands
respect by never demanding it—
she lives with intention.

she is nurturing.

Every day I am aware that I do not walk alone. My ancestors grace me—those women that turned *can't* into *can.* To the world they were never valued—generally dismissed and demeaned to a life of servitude. These women were always more that the acts they performed: washing, cooking, and cleaning—taking care of somebody else's children. They had their own dreams and many times those dreams went unfulfilled. These women were beauty, strength and love incarnate. They were also more: thinkers, lovers, fighters and philosophers. When I speak in the language of poetry, I know that their acts inspire and accompany my voice. I do not speak alone. My verse is joined by the unheard multitudes, the women that could not write their own stories. In my poems, I channel their voices that shake the foundation of the earth with soul. When I sit still, I feel them move. Then, I do their bidding. I put pen to paper and then I write to right wrongs.

-Glenis Redmond

The cure for anything is salt water—tears, sweat or the sea.

-ISAK DINESEN

What makes you worthwhile is who you are, not what you do.

-MARIANNE WILLIAMS

Listening, not imitation, may be the sincerest form of flattery.

-JOYCE BROTHERS

The excursion is the same when you go looking for your sorrow as when you go looking for your joy.

-EUDORA WELTY

It took me a long time not to judge myself through someone else's eyes.

-SALLY FIELD

Always be a first rate version of yourself, instead of a second rate version of somebody else.

-JUDY GARLAND

Prove to yourself that you can do it. Prove that you were always who you thought you were, not who they said you had to be.

-RACHEL SNYDER

Dear Generous Heart,

In the quiet moments, those sweet times or pauses in which you feel your weariness, you might wonder what it is you have left to give. Hear, then, the whisper of your own support system, the legacy which comes of your many miles, like a wind down a deep canyon,

"You have everything you need. Begin again, nurture your own garden. It is from that growing abundance that you are able to provide hope to others."

Has it been some time since someone let you know they appreciate you? Do you remember the last time someone observed how your action of lifting others up seems to make you happy? I know you've explained in so many different ways that when you raise someone up—you raise yourself up right alongside them. You know, in your heart, that the nurturing doesn't start outside yourself. Of course you are strong for others, because you embrace your own fortitude. You provide solid direction because you frequently recalibrate your own compass. Keep checking—you hold your own true north.

With much love.

She is prepared for the serendipity a journey delivers. She sees with "first time eyes" and allows familiar paths to become new adventures.

She is undeterred by delay and trusts to right timing for all her connections. She is fierce and fearless.

She is always moments away from being packed and ready to go. She understands where she thinks she is headed might not be where she ends up.

Each time she prepares for a departure she hauls less and is ready to learn more.

she is an intrepid traveler.

I once believed I traveled for the adventure, for the discoveries about myself and the world. That was part of it. These aspects of travel fed me. But today I pack my bag and follow a new route because of the extremes it presents. For the deep, dark of night in the desert, or the screaming bright of northern sunrise. For the wild joy of families dancing through a marriage, or the somber, heavy moments shared in the wake of war. For when I feel empowered and tall on a mountain top, to when I feel broken and tired. I walk toward these extremes that challenge, make me question, make me stand up and notice. And then somewhere along the path, I shift from that extreme anticipation of the next new place to its contrast, and the warm and welcome call of home.

-Gina Bramucci

Difficult situations can sometimes beckon us to share our humanity with the world, complete with its stunning array of imperfections and vivid display of unique responses to tough times.

-DEANNA DAVIS, PH.D.

It is good to have an end to journey towards, but it is the journey that matters, in the end.

-URSULA K. LEGUIN

I am not the same having seen the moon shine on the other side of the world.

-MARY ANNE RADMACHER

Nothing's far when one wants to get there.

-QUEEN MARIE OF ROMANIA

Knowledge alters what we seek as well as what we find.

-FREDA ADLER

I have no home but me.

-ANNE TRUITT

The impulse to travel is one of the hopeful symptoms of life.

-AGNES REPPLIER

Travel is as much a passion as ambition or love.

-L.E. LANDON

Dear Wide-Eyed One,

You carry your sense of home within you. There are times when you want to just fold yourself into the familiar. Travel offers lots of first times and elegant uncertainties. Sometimes you just want to do something so known to you that it could be accomplished without a second thought.

In the midst of unrecognized views, and roads you have yet to see it is a comfort to remember that all the roads do ultimately lead you home. It's a sweet knowing you hold—confident that after a short time with habit and pattern you will be ready for another adventure. Cherish the transition times, the crossroads, the intersections. Cherish them all for the instructive gift of memory they become once you have finished one road.

May the wind fill your sail and may you have a following sea,

she

she is smart. she is sassy. she is silly. she is sophisticated and magnificent. she has been known to be mistaken for a fairy, most often by children. Adults simply find her enchanting.

There is nothing in her world that is considered old or is discarded. she helps craft things and people into their true purpose. she is magical, she is mesmerizing. she loves music AND she can dance. she's awesome.

she is magical.

I dance because I can. You can, too. Hear the music? It's underfoot. And overhead. And inside you. Listen carefully; it's always there. You've got all the moves, step aside. Turn. Lean in. Yield. Circle Back. Spin around. Bend over backwards. Lean forward. Rest assured. Scoot over. Cozy up. Move closer. Dance your work, dance your play, dance your heartbreak, dance your joy.

-Kathleen Gallagher Everett

Keep dreaming your dream, stay true to yourself, choose the path of faith over fear.

-JILL BADONSKY

We should see dreaming as one of our responsibilities, rather than an alternative to one.

-MARY ENGELBREIT

Some things have to be believed to be seen.

-MADELEINE L'ENGLE

You have power. You are the magic wand.

-LAURA SCHLESSINGER

A good cook is like a sorceress who dispenses happiness.

-ELSA SCHIAPARELLI

Goals are dreams with deadlines.

-DIANA SCHARF HUNT

To dance is to be out of yourself. Larger, more beautiful, more powerful. This is power; it is glory on earth; and it is yours for the taking.

-AGNES DE MILLE

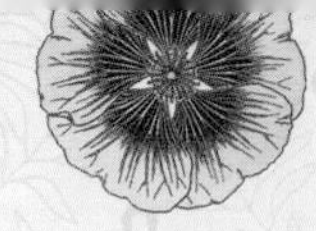

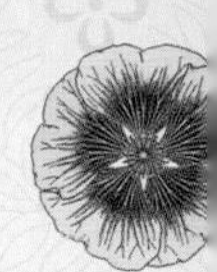

Dear Magical One—

Your capacity for both the stunning and the subtle is awe-inspiring. So often your gentle, lyrical whisper proves more compelling than the most audacious announcement. Even animals willingly follow you, apparently intrigued by what they will hear next.

Your ability to discern the proper and healing moments to invite stillness and silence must account, at least in small part, for your reserve of energy. While others lament that they must "Sit this one out," you still dance. And dance some more. It's wonderful.

One of the most magical things about you is your well placed use of "I'm sorry." It springs from an intuitive place of sympathy. Your movements come from such integrity that you rarely are called to offer apology for your actions.

Your feet are rooted in an ethical garden and you thrive making service and efficiency look every bit like play. You've assured many that baking forty-eight homemade cherry pies is a festivity when it's done with love and gratitude. Ah—the love and gratitude element. A real key to your magic.

With appreciation—

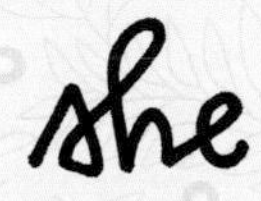

she is quiet and she is observant.

she is a warrior (although you have to know her to believe it). she plans and prepares while recognizing chaos is inevitable.

In the face of uncertainty, she organizes her pen drawer and then moves forward with fierce tenacity.

she does not take a chance on whim but measures the potentials of remaining safe against the outcomes of her long-held vision. she speculates on loss in order to press forward with the passion that animates her actions. she is not reckless—

she is a purposeful risk taker.

When I started my business (Quotable) with my partner, Matt, we really went with our gut instincts. I knew then and even more, now, that when your "gut" tells you something is a good idea, and tells you *strongly*, you'd better not ignore it. I DID go with my gut—but I didn't just drop everything and "go for it." I was systematic. I broke the idea down into tangible tasks and kept the other parts of my life and work intact while pursuing this gut feeling. I followed the idea in evenings, and during my free time. In that way it was a calculated risk, a safe risk for me. It didn't put me AT risk. In that way, I was able to feel excited and fully present (not panicked) while creating the structure that is now a recognizable brand all over the world. Being purposeful was, and still is, a big part of my being a risk-taker.

-Gillian Simon

Your wings already exist. All you have to do is be willing to spread them open.

-CHRISTINE MASON MILLER

If you obey all the rules you miss all the fun.

-KATHARINE HEPBURN

The reward for conformity is that everyone likes you but yourself.

-RITA MAE BROWN

One way to open your eyes is to ask yourself, "What if I had never seen this before? What if I knew I would never see it again?"

-RACHEL CARSON

Every society honors its live conformists and its dead troublemakers.

-MIGNON MCLAUGHLIN

Failure is just another opportunity to learn how to do something right.

-MARIAN WRIGHT EDELMAN

I am never afraid of what I know.

-ANNA SEWELL

If you don't risk anything, you risk even more.

-ERICA JONG

Dear Dauntless One,

I'm tempted to tease you about your "risky business," but I can't—your risks seem to always be tied with the safe ribbons of purpose and planning. Of course I gasp, we all do, when you step off that ledge. From behind it looks terrifying. We've come to understand that you will have already put in place ladders, ropes and nets. Brilliant.

You possess a fierce tenacity that your quietness does not immediately reflect. I think of that time when we were kids and you quietly made your way to the deep end of the pool and climbed the highest diving board. I thought for sure your mom was going to leap into the water with her clothes on. But she held her breath and watched. We all did. Nobody had noticed that you'd taught yourself to swim in the shallow end. All those weeks we were busy playing water soccer you were gaining mad skills.

What a surprise you are. You just keep on pondering the hard questions of life, please. We have been schooled enough to know that when your soft voice delivers an answer—we had better listen.

Wow, how very much you are admired.

she integrates ideas and is at ease with the "we" over the "me." she assimilates without having her identity absorbed. she values combination over competition. she is as interested in the contribution of the other as she is in her own. she has the confidence to cocreate. she shares the burdens and benefits, works toward a mutual vision and participates in shared responsibility.

she trusts. she says what is true. she keeps her promises.

she remembers the reasons for her commitments and they inspire her, even when she's weary.

she is cooperative
and collaborative.

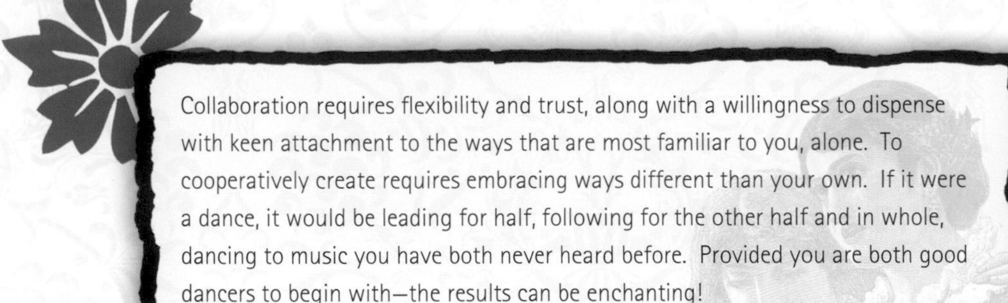

Collaboration requires flexibility and trust, along with a willingness to dispense with keen attachment to the ways that are most familiar to you, alone. To cooperatively create requires embracing ways different than your own. If it were a dance, it would be leading for half, following for the other half and in whole, dancing to music you have both never heard before. Provided you are both good dancers to begin with—the results can be enchanting!

-Mary Anne Radmacher

Cooperation and collaboration are about joining our voices to create a collective sound; neither holding back nor needing to overshadow the other voice(s). Think of the grace and the beauty and the power that come form a chorus of voices, how the sound washes over you, and how you can hear your own voice joined in harmony with others—truly a miracle.

-Liz Kalloch

Whatever our souls are made of, his and mine are the same.

-EMILY BRONTË

Surround yourself with only people who are going to lift you higher.

-OPRAH WINFREY

To handle yourself, use your head; to handle others, use your heart.

-ELEANOR ROOSEVELT

Lots of people want to ride with you in the limo, but what you want is someone who will take the bus with you when the limo breaks down.

-OPRAH WINFREY

Cooperation is the thorough conviction that nobody can get there unless everybody gets there.

-VIRGINIA BURDEN TOWER

The one thing that doesn't abide by majority rule is a person's conscience.

-HARPER LEE

The one hand trying to wash itself is a pitiful spectacle, but when one hand washes the other, power is increased and it becomes a force to be reckoned with.

-MAYA ANGELOU

What we have to do...is to find a way to celebrate our diversity and debate our differences without fracturing our communities.

-HILLARY RODHAM CLINTON

Dear Friend:

Doing almost anything with a good friend makes it seem more fun. The time seems to tick away more quickly when working with kindred spirits. Working together toward a mutually valued goal elevates the action. Whatever that action might be—from a girl's afternoon out to preservation wild lands to serving hungry families. You are not alone. You are in community—part of something bigger.

Trusting partners in possibility with your truth is a significant element to collaboration. Face judgments and assumptions squarely and in a timely manner. They sneak in. Set aside concern regarding expressing yourself with candor. You are a contributor—and you get to bring your whole true self to the party.

If there's consequence to articulating yourself, with integrity, you will work through it. We can be stronger, together. And that requires you bring your personal strength as an important ingredient. You can't keep a solid grasp on what is being collectively created. Pitch in and let go. Bring your best to the effort and trust for the best outcomes.

Here's to saying, "Yes!"

she

she suspects her capacity and she embraces her fragility.

she embraces the contradictions of anger and action, of
memory and hope, of weariness and unflagging enthusiasm.
she allows her body to be a door of knowing.

she listens. she learns to listen more deeply each time she
practices movement, chops wood, creates anything and
comforts those ravaged by war, loss or the flu.
she is familiar with despair, sleeplessness and is
unafraid of sadness. she welcomes those difficult
visitors as teachers as well as her joys and epiphanies.

she speaks up, readily, for others and for herself.

she walks, wanders and tells the stories
she knows, gently.

she is compassionate.

Ever since I was a girl, I've searched for a religion to call my own. I spent many hours praying and searching holy texts for a faith that could match the love and concern I felt for all beings everywhere. Later I searched for a secular code to live by, studying ethics and human rights. I put those theories to the test, living in war zones reknowned for moral complexity and ethical ambiguity. I discovered that in times of uncertainty, confusion, anger or grief—kindness mattered more than ever. Finally it became clear: in the words of the Dalai Lama, compassion is "my simple religion." Albert Einstein wrote that in order to free ourselves, we must widen our circle of compassion to all living creatures. As I have learned, our compassion must embrace even our messy, flawed selves. "Be kind," said Plato, "for everyone you meet is fighting a hard battle." My daily lesson is to remember that I too am often fighting a hard battle, and compassion is my greatest source of strength and sustenance as well as the best gift I can offer the world.

-Marianne Elliott

I've learned that people will forget what you said, people will forget what you did, but people will never forget how you made them feel.

-MAYA ANGELOU

It is by spending oneself that one becomes rich.

-SARAH BERNHARDT

So often we think we have got to make a difference and be a big dog. Let us just try to be little fleas biting. Enough fleas biting strategically can make a big dog very uncomfortable.

-MARIAN WRIGHT EDELMAN

The total history of almost anyone would shock almost everyone.

-MIGNON MCLAUGHLIN

I prefer you to make mistakes in kindness than work miracles in unkindness.

-MOTHER TERESA

My feeling is that there is nothing in life but refraining from hurting others, and comforting those that are sad.

-OLIVE SCHREINER

Flowers grow out of dark moments.

-CORITA KENT

Dear Compassionate Caretaker,

They say the sea can never be poured full. The needs and injustices of the world, from your backyard to beyond the borders of your country, seem an endless, rising tide. You are moved to tears by the resilience of the human spirit, seized with anger at inequities and then you choose your action.

Will you simply weep and water the garden of your tender concern? Pray? Light a candle? March? Sign a petition? Offer sustaining support? The choices themselves can seem overwhelming. That immediate response of, "What can I do?" is at the core of compassion. Shepherding your reserves: it's an important part of reaching out. You know you cannot do everything or be everywhere.

Being present in the moment, wherever you are, deepens your ability to listen to yourself. "No, not today, not you," to "Yes, now is the time and you are the one." Remember and be confident that your "No," becomes the opportunity for someone else's "Yes." Be assured, even though it appears otherwise, your efforts matter. They make a difference, because you, Sweet One, make a difference. Rest deeply: let it pour you full, restoring your capacity to extend your hand. Again. And, then, again.

Be good to yourself.

she

she knows what's important. she is masterful. she never seems to hurry and yet all her "everything" seems to get done. she has a tremendous capacity for detail. she remembers. especially she remembers the names of children. she considers every person she meets a possible instrument for the greater good.

she's artful in the way she effortlessly combines seemingly contradictory parts. she assists others as they seek answers by helping them ask the right questions. she reads. she learns. she listens. she loves her friends as much as she loves her books.

she is resourceful.

"Diplomacy is not something that is confined to the State Department or reserved for special occasions. In this complicated, connected world, diplomacy is a daily practical occurrence. It's about people learning from each other and building understandings through the kinds of interactions that happen millions of times each day in person and online. In fact, I think we need to practice diplomacy from the lunch table to the board room to the government offices."

-Hillary Rodham Clinton, January 30, 2013

To know how to do something well is to enjoy it.

-PEARL S. BUCK

Love as much as you can from where you are with what you've got. That's the best you can ever do.

-CHERI HUBER

We gain power in our refusal to accept less than we deserve.

-AMBER HOLLIBAUGH

Nothing strengthens the judgment and quickens the conscience like individual responsibility.

-ELIZABETH CADY STANTON

Alpha women—are astonishingly energetic, and have a gift for taking charge and getting things done. But they are not driven by a desire for power or a need to dominate others, but by clarity of vision, resoluteness of purpose and a delight in accomplishment. Their need to govern does not apply to people but to circumstances.

-ANNE GIARDINI

The impossible talked of is less impossible from the moment words are laid to it.

-STORM JAMESON

Common sense is seeing things as they are and doing things as they ought to be.

-HARRIET BEECHER STOWE

Dear Unflappable One,

You are one of those who experience no degree of separation when it comes to solving problems. You remember names, you collect contacts and business cards knowing they are currency for a cause. You are utterly engaged in a broad selection of activities. Your connection to and understanding of your priorities casts a wide net—harvesting support and enthusiasm.

In addition to idea-gathering, you build consensus and break barriers. A grasp of history intersects with an improbable sense of possibilities—to produce assistance, resources and measurable results. A unique sense of drive defines you.

Those who do not see you correctly describe it as cold ambition, or an inability to stop working. Those who know understand your sight for Great Solutions is what spurs you onward.

Please write yourself a note—a reminder that self care allows you to better care for others. Only you know when it must be time for you to pause. As you roundly consider the highest and best use of each of your 24 hours, a gentle reach to a friend is high on your list. You know what's really important and each day you demand of yourself that you act accordingly.

Be well.

she

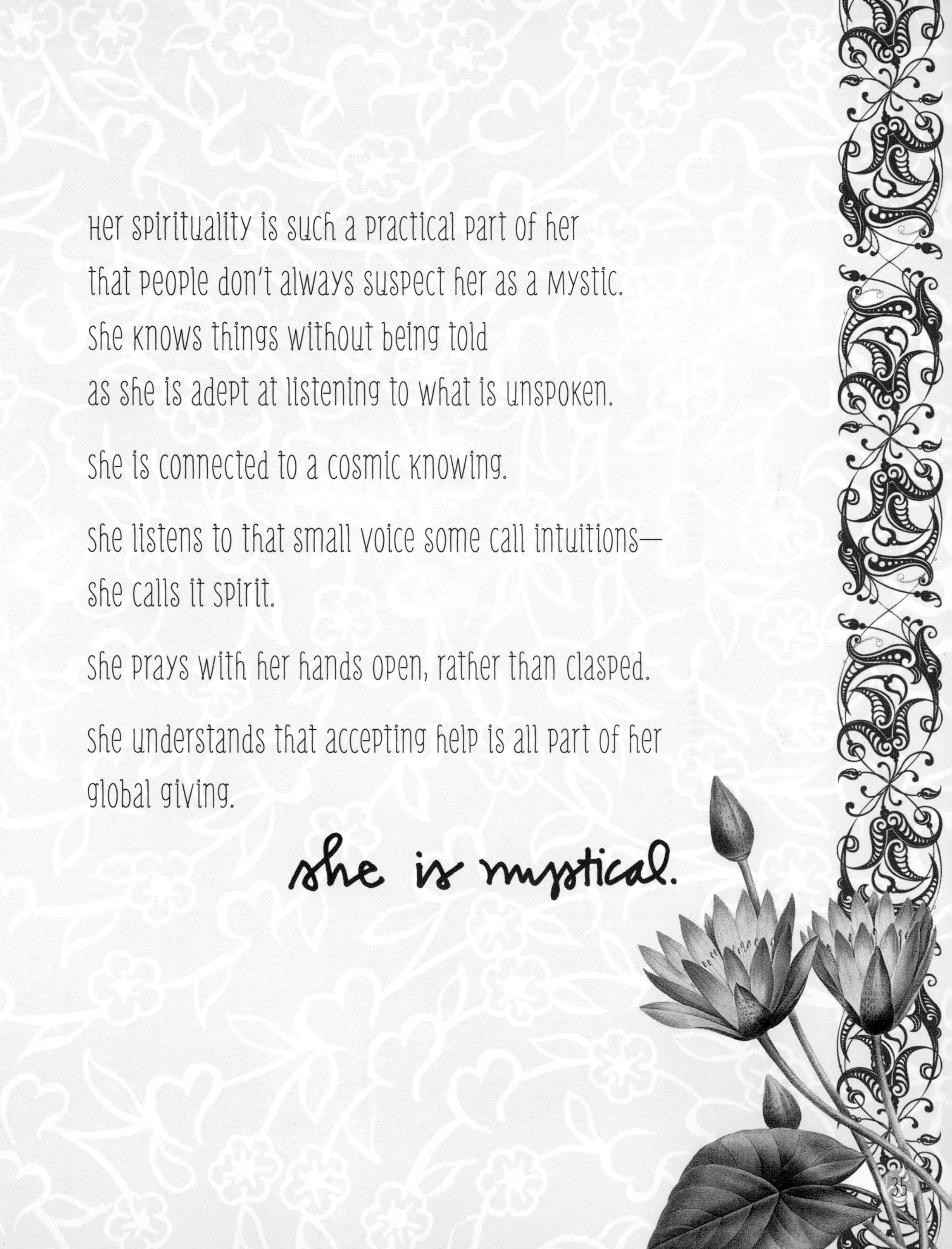

Her spirituality is such a practical part of her
that people don't always suspect her as a mystic.
She knows things without being told
as she is adept at listening to what is unspoken.

She is connected to a cosmic knowing.

She listens to that small voice some call intuitions—
she calls it spirit.

She prays with her hands open, rather than clasped.

She understands that accepting help is all part of her
global giving.

she is mystical.

Every woman has the capacity to call upon her mystical self, the keeper of her sacred worlds within. This secret sanctuary shows us how to navigate the domains of spirit and form. From these visits, we pull the red thread of mystery that we use to weave the fabric of our lives. A vital, self-expressed life includes an integration of these two worlds. This is where the magic happens. To allow these chambers within us to be hidden or fragmented from our daily lives can result in a loss of our core identity. It is possible to be enchanted, and to be in love with the world, but we have to choose. Through the integration of this mystical self into our ordinary reality we make what the Shamans call "non-ordinary reality." This mystic well is the place where the creatives draw forth their inspiration. It is here that I access what longs to be expressed and enter into the mystic.

-Shiloh McCloud

Let nothing dim the light that shines from within.

-MAYA ANGELOU

One way to open your eyes is to ask yourself, "What if I had never seen this before? What if I knew I would never see it again?"

-RACHEL CARSON

I think this sanctuary must be the kind of place where very unsuspectingly we meet God face to face.

-HELEN STEINER RICE

Find out who you are and be that person. That's what your soul was put on this earth to be. Find that truth, live that truth and everything else will come.

-ELLEN DEGENERES

People who keep journals have life twice.

-JESSAMYN WEST

In every human breast, God has implanted a Principle, which we call Love of Freedom; it is impatient of Oppression, and pants for Deliverance.

-PHILLIS WHEATLEY

There is no unbelief; whoever plants a seed beneath a sod and waits to see it push away the clod, He trusts in God.

-LIZZIE YORK CASE

Instinct is the nose of the mind.

-DELPHINE DE GIRARDIN

Dear Divine Dancer,

You dwell in a state that few have the courage to visit for long. You live in a land populated by symbol, imagery, icon, vivid imaginings. You are often alone but rarely lonely. The cadence of the sea striking shore is an orchestration to you; it calls you to remember a primal dance. And you will dance, with the comfort of your tribe or in the valleys and thoroughfares of people not yet known.

You do not answer to the clamor of approval but to the affirming assessment of resonant truth in your spirit. Wear your choices as an honor and consider your differing ways as homage to the dreamers, the vision questers who have gone before you. There is a demanding passion within you that would burst apart if you did not give it voice, allow it movement, provide it paint, allow its words to be recounted in story.

Your narrative becomes a glimpse of inspiration to any who have the nerve to listen. That tale is one of a richer way of being, the capacity to sing a song that is true, in every note. Wrap yourself in the colorful garments of your knowing and may your strength be long in your dance.

Others can see because you believe.

she

she discovers the sound of her heart, every day.

she teaches, she sings. she stares in the mirror and dares herself to say what is true in that moment. she feels the burden of those who are silent and long to speak up, not only for herself, but for others.

she has the grace to grasp and welcome the role of silence. she speaks purposefully and values meaning over speed. she understands communication of any type originates in her core but it thrives in community.

she has the courage to take her voice to the larger space. she makes her mark by making a sound. sometimes it is a short shout and other times it is a lyrical whisper. the sound, regardless of volume or context, is always one of her own making.

she has a voice.

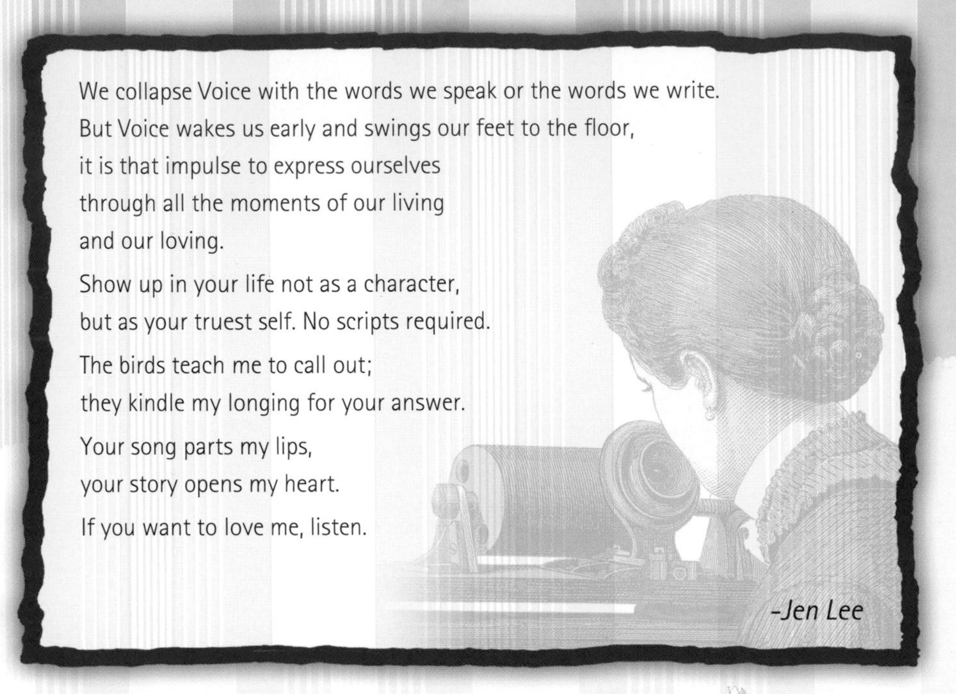

We collapse Voice with the words we speak or the words we write.
But Voice wakes us early and swings our feet to the floor,
it is that impulse to express ourselves
through all the moments of our living
and our loving.

Show up in your life not as a character,
but as your truest self. No scripts required.

The birds teach me to call out;
they kindle my longing for your answer.

Your song parts my lips,
your story opens my heart.

If you want to love me, listen.

–Jen Lee

These precious gifts we give to the world simply by being ourselves.

-CHRISTINE MASON MILLER

I'm tough, I'm ambitious, and I know exactly what I want. If that makes me a bitch, okay.

-MADONNA

Polite conversation is rarely either.

-FRAN LEBOWITZ

There are many strong voices, there are many kinds of strong voices. Surely there should be room for all.

-MARGARET ATWOOD

I am delighted daily by the intimacy of voice.

-ELEANOR WACHTEL

Hello, you, with Magnificent Messages,

You have always suspected that having a voice had nothing to do with being heard above the crowd but that it means having something significant to say. You know the anxiety of second-guessing your own silence with, "If only I'd spoken up."

Speaking up for yourself is ideal training for speaking up for those who cannot yet, or ever speak for themselves. When events conspire to erase our presence or to constrain your words, stand firm. Your feet are firmly fixed and you observe. Be a witness and be able to tell and recount. This is so important to you, The Voice. First you See before you Speak.

You will never be made invisible because of the strength of your tell. Whether it issues forth as a shout or a stutter, your words are proof. Demonstration that you are here. You will stand. On those days when you shake a little, your advocates put their hands to your shoulders. Together you raise your voices. It can even sound like a song.

Keep singing.

she is both elegant and outrageous. she wears her own style with strength and dignity. her shoes are the envy of all. she inspires first herself and then others.

In her vulnerability she shows that inspiration does not equal perfection but rather being true to your own knowing is what makes every moment "just perfect."

she cries as easily as she laughs and sometimes for the exact same reason. she is unique, authentic and utterly enjoys being herself.

she is inspiring.

The word origin for outrageous is "excessive or extravagant." And the word inspiration comes from the Latin root "inspirare," which means "to inhale or breathe in." Outrageous inspiration—extravagant breath. What a concept! The practice of embracing the exquisite in each moment with no regard for limits or conventions, offering no apologies, only authenticity. The unabashed basking in life's grand journey. The blissful, full-body stretch into the newness of each day, paired with a luxurious, purposeful, passionate sigh. And then, "YES!" Inhale. Explore. Uplift. Evolve. Be. Outrageous inspiration—extravagant breath, indeed.

-Deanna Davis

It is not necessary, or desirable, to try to become someone you think is better than the way you are.

-CHERI HUBER

The only way to cope with something deadly serious is to try to treat it a little lightly.

-MADELEINE L'ENGLE

The most beautiful thing in the world is, precisely, the conjunction of learning and inspiration.

-WANDA LANDOWSKA

Adornment is never anything except a reflection of the heart.

-GABRIELLE "COCO" CHANEL

Fashion can be bought. Style one must possess.

-EDNA WOOLMAN CHASE

Oh, never mind the fashion. When one has a style of one's own, it is always twenty times better.

-MARGARET OLIPHANT

Just don't give up trying to do what you really want to do. Where there is love and inspiration, I don't think you can go wrong.

-ELLA FITZGARALD

Beauty is about being comfortable in your own skin. It's about knowing and accepting who you are.

-ELLEN DEGENERES

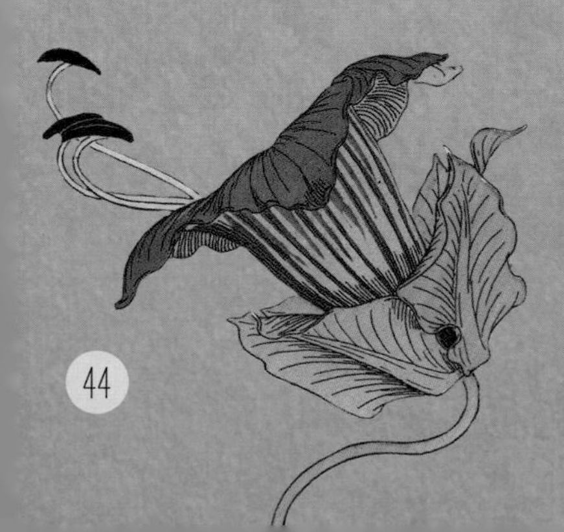

Dear Dreamer of Infinite Dreams,

While you may have said that you wouldn't repeat the sorts of things your parents said to you...there's one phrase I hope you'll hold on to and fully embrace.

"Because I said so."

This is the answer to many things. That occasional self doubt. That persistent second-guessing. Look the uncertainties asserting themselves square in the eye and enunciate, "Because. I. Said. So." The value of this phrase extends beyond the realm of self-talk. Vividly connecting to your own inspired actions seems to invite a raft of nay-sayers and dream slayers. They ask questions that sound like, "Really? You're going to do THAT?" or "Oh, that's interesting. Are you trained for that?"

When your own sense of knowing is called to someone else's spotlight—that's when a healthy does of "because I said so," (also easily remembered as BISS) really serves the conversation. At the end of the matter, any matter, there's one expert on the subject of your personal passions, longings and vision. That, my dearest, is YOU. Remember the phrase when addressing doubt, any doubt, yours or someone else's. Knowing what is true for you, doesn't have to be true for anyone else, is sometimes knowing enough. And, please, while you are remembering, continue remembering to breathe deeply.

Inspired by you,

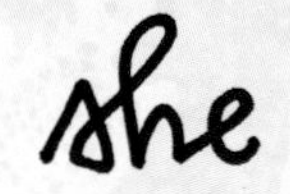

she is a reason to celebrate. she is a joy. she wears laughter as if it were her favorite dress. she brings sunshine into any room. she knows sadness well and in fact, they have an odd friendship. she believes that familiarity with certain sorrows is what gives her the lofty view into her zippy peace of mind.

It is the diverse contrasts in her life that provide her so many reasons to be in bliss. contrasts that sound like, "Life is too serious to be taken seriously." she knows the secret to the best kind of life is knowing when to giggle.

she is happy.

Happiness is sitting at our bedside like a pair of sparkly rimmed glasses, begging us to wear it each morning and see life through its lenses. Happiness wants to hold hands with us and let it be our tour guide through life, showing us all of the things we weren't seeing back when we thought we weren't happy. Happiness is constantly calling out to us..."Choose me! Choose me! Choose me!" Happiness has nothing to do with a golden ticket that only the lucky ones find, but really a choice to see the golden moments all around us and to make more golden moments every chance we get. May we ALL choose happiness.

-Melody Ross

Keeping busy and making optimism a way of life can restore your faith in yourself.

-LUCILLE BALL

You lose a lot of time hating people.

-MARIAN ANDERSON

Your life can be different in any moment you choose to change your choices.

-CHERI HUBER

When I lay my head on the pillow at night I can say I was a decent person today. That's when I feel beautiful.

-DREW BARRYMORE

There are shortcuts to happiness, and dancing is one of them.

-VICKI BAUM

The dance is a poem of which each movement is a word.

-MATA HARI

If you have enough butter, anything is good.

-JULIA CHILD

The big secret in life is that there is no big secret. Whatever your goal, you can get there if you're willing to work.

-OPRAH WINFREY

There can be no happiness if the things we believe in are different than the things we do.

-FREYA STARK

Sweet, Cheerful One:

I always appreciate your happy, buoyant manner. You have a way about you that just makes me feel tickled pink and downright blissful. I want to be clear—I do not take your happiness for granted. No, I do not. I know the laws of physics and there are times, certainly, when your rapturous pendulum of joy swings over the moon and comes down on the other side of happy. Those times? They support and inform the delight. They, by means of contrast, allow you to know and celebrate all the various clouds all the way to cloud nine.

Those moments when your bounce is bounced out and you have little jump left—much less jumping for joy—those times are important in the larger picture of things. They sharpen your compassionate edge, they give you strength for some and patience for others. One of the things that is most treasured in you is that even in the midst of your dark night of the soul, you appreciate the beauty of the moon. And that thread of appreciation guides you back to the place where it is you doing all the beaming and the shining.

Your kind, sweet ways brighten and lighten roads of people you don't even know and waters so many gardens in the world. Gardens whose blooms you have invited and do not often get to smell or enjoy. And that you are okay with that is one of the many reasons I love being in your company. Everyone who knows you has their own reasons and I'm thankful you provide so many opportunities to be adored.

Just thinking of you puts me in good spirits,

she

She has breadth of skill and impulse. From an internal diversity she partners what she expresses with what she experiences.

She takes joy from helping others do the same.

She appreciates the need for rest. She knows a natural pause is what waters possibility. It can appear as hesitation to others but she knows it as prudent consideration. She recognizes punctuation as a natural metaphor for life processes.

She functions within the hyphenated thought, stops a beat after a comma and braves the spaces after a semicolon. She uses her skills to walk, to ride, to sojourn and listen to all the songs of the world. In listening she is stirred to contribute.

she embodies actions and words.

UNTO OTHERS AS YOU WOULD THAT THEY SHOULD
LOVE ONE ANOTHER

I am drawn to the wildly improbable, the whoosh of big dreaming, that drop in my gut that gifts me a glimpse of my own daring imagination and the stubborn desire I carry within me to actualize it. What makes me come alive is the invitation to investigate and challenge boundaries and to nourish my life with creative journeys that rarely have templates, guidelines or guardrails. I've discovered that pursuing this path requires patience, deep listening, trust, and self-compassion; it is not easy to bridge the gap between birthing dreams and shepherding them into action—so much doubt creeps in, along with fear, anxiety, feelings of scarcity and isolation, and a heightened (and disproportionate) self-criticism. Writing—grounding my ideas in poems, stories, and other narratives—helps me find the threadlines and throughways and gives me the great permission slip I need to find the courage to move forward.

-Maya Stein

I've always roared with laughter when they say life begins at forty. That's the funniest remark ever. The day I was born was when life began for me.

-BETTE DAVIS

If you can't change your fate, change your attitude.

-AMY TAN

Clinging to the past is the problem. Embracing change is the solution.

-GLORIA STEINEM

Dreams are…illustrations from the book your soul is writing about you.

-MARSHA NORMAN

We have too many high sounding words and too few actions that correspond with them.

-ABIGAIL ADAMS

Being told to sit still and enjoy myself is logically incompatible.

-LESLIE GLENDOWER PEABODY

A word is dead when it is said, some say. I say it just begins to live that day.

-EMILY DICKINSON

Greetings Great Synthesizer of Words and Works,

I know you smile, ever so slightly, where you hear this beginning, "Oh, HERE's an idea that would be great for you to do." Inevitably what will follow is a set of things, not necessarily in any particular (logical) order of all things for you to do to complete this great idea. It's simply part of your lot in life. I've watched you learn so many gracious ways to invite those idea-sharers to act on an impulse for themselves. You! You make the awesome and close-to-impossible look so easy. You not only talk about great ideas, sharing your visions and ideas with candor and willing vulnerability, you turn around and act on them. Whooosh... words and works working together. It's stunning, really. So you can't blame the masses for feeding you concepts and promises that they haven't the courage to implement themselves.

It seems like those passed along ideas have given you a deeper understanding that not all ideas are meant to be acted upon. The job of some ideas is to burn out and in their smoke and embers give birth to something else. Sort of like the legend of the phoenix. The ashes of the "didn't work" ideas produce a new spark that ignites a brand new action. And it appears so natural when you do it. I love that about you.

I think you are one of the people who inspire others to say such things as, "She walks her talk," and "She practices what she preaches." You do. And shhhhhh. You are under no obligation to tell anyone about those six days that you did nothing but watch re-runs, old movies and eat root beer floats. Oh, how like you. You'll tell on yourself, even if no one asks. Because that's part of the deal, isn't it? You know that sometimes you don't act on the grand plan and at certain times you break a promise you made to yourself. It all works into the greater scheme of things. How would you know what combining the power of intending and doing looks like if you didn't also know what it doesn't look like? It's encouraging that you accept that as part of the equation.

You are good at swinging between the idea and the action. And you somehow manage to rest and make healthy choices in the course of that swinging. Oh, thank you. You manage to incorporate consistency without making it look predictable or feel boring.

Inspired to greater heights,

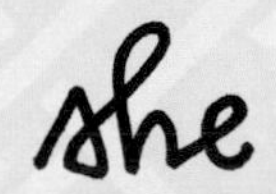

She practices the difference between being still and remaining silent. She demonstrates the difference between being utterly engaged in the moment and being busy b-u-s-y BUSY!

Her words and what she does are agents of change that she uses with the precision of weaponry and the effectiveness of healing herbs.

She takes note of the opinion of others and guides her path by the illuminating light of her own moon and sun.

She is loved by children and respected by adults. She is authentic. She is surprisingly funny. She does what is necessary to answer the demands of her calling.

she is regal.

"There is no doubt, if you aim high enough, that you will be confronted by those who say that your efforts to change the world or improve the lot of those around you do not mean much in the grand scheme of things. But no matter how impotent you may sometimes feel, have courage still—and persevere. It is certain, if you aim high enough, that you will find your strongest beliefs ridiculed and challenged; principles that you cherish may be derisively dismissed by those claiming to be more practical or realistic than you. But no matter how weary you may become in persuading others to see the value in what you value, have courage still—and persevere. Inevitably, if you aim high enough, you will be buffeted by demands of family, friends and employment that will conspire to distract you from your course. But no matter how difficult it may be to meet the commitments you have made, have courage still—and persevere. It has been said that all work that is worth anything is done in faith. I summon you... to embrace the faith that your courage and your perseverance will make a difference; and that every life enriched by your giving, every friend touched by your affection, every soul inspired by your passion and every barrier to justice brought down by your determination, will ennoble your own life, inspire others, serve your country, and explode outward the boundaries of what is achievable on this earth."

-Madeleine K. Albright
Commencement Address, Mount Holyoke College, May 25, 1997

Being powerful is like being a lady. If you have to tell people you are, you aren't.

-MARGARET THATCHER

Never interrupt someone doing what you said couldn't be done.

-AMELIA EARHART

It's a rare thing, graciousness. The shape of it can be acquired, but not, I think, the substance.

-GERTRUDE SCHWEITZER

If you are not your own agent, you are someone else's.

-ALICE MOLLOY

Oh, Stately Sister—

You are a model of self-sustaining service. You help others recognize there comes a time when the answers you provide your own questioning heart are more important than the assumptions or assertions of others: Big people protect little ones. Those who have a voice speak up for those that cannot speak for themselves. Those who have been helped—helped others. Justice is not based on popular notions but on time-honored principles. We are not isolated, solitary individuals but rather we are a part of an ever-widening community. You prove, over and over again, we live in a circle not a line.

With great admiration,

she

she lifts others up. she accepts praise as easily as she gives it. she leads, teaches and guides. she follows, learns and walks beside her friends on any adventure.

she values the metaphor of a mirror—she holds it facing inward to reflect her own knowing. she faces it outward to help others recognize themselves. she creates and ponders excellent questions. when she asks a question of someone else, she listens hard to the answer. she knows listening does not equal agreeing. she is confident enough to disagree, without being disagreeable.

she's courageous and never uses the word, "failure,"—she just tries another way. she is admired and has the grace to be embraced.

she is a leader.

When I invite you to my home for dinner, if you get lost on the way, is it better to tell you how to get here from where *you* are or where *I* am? Obviously I need to tell you how to get here from where *you* are. And that is what a leader does. They don't stand in their rightness or vision and demand you see it and navigate from their vantage point. They come where you are, and travel with you.

-Patti Digh

What better gift can we give our children than ourselves in all our glory?

-ALEXANDRA STODDARD

I am not afraid of storms for I am learning how to sail my ship.

-LOUISA MAY ALCOTT

The speed of the leader is the speed of the gang.

-MARY KAY ASH

To be alive is to be vulnerable.

-MADELEINE L'ENGLE

Life is a verb, not a noun.

-CHARLOTTE PERKINS GILMAN

I have always thought that what is needed is the development of people who are interested not in being leaders as much as in developing leadership in others.

-ELLA J. BAKER

Leadership should be born out of the understanding of the needs of those who would be affected by it.

-MARIAN ANDERSON

Ninety percent of leadership is the ability to communicate something people want.

-DIANNE FEINSTEIN

The uplift of a fearless heart will help us over barriers. No one ever overcomes difficulties by going at them in a hesitant, doubtful way.

-LAURA INGALLS WILDER

The right way is not always the popular and easy way. Standing for right when it is unpopular is a true test of moral character.

-MARGARET CHASE SMITH

Greetings, Pathfinder!

You've been listening to your heart and following your own bliss since you were little. Back in the day it surprised you to glance behind you and see the number of people there, coming after you. You might even have asked, "Why do you want to do what I'm doing?" It puzzled you then. And, still, sometimes, you are startled at the number of people who want to do what you are doing. You've learned that the mantle of leadership lies in not allowing people to simply do what you do. You are a model but more importantly, you demonstrate the ways to find their own ways. You school them, "This is MY way: this is the way I found it. These are tools that may or may not work for you. Try. Explore. Consider. Always, always the objective is to find the way to your own way." Then, once those who look to you for leadership choose their route...you challenge them to own it. Own the path and light it up to make a clear way for others. You know that the key to leadership isn't that you inspire those behind you to follow you...but that you inspire them to lead others to their own journeys.

With marvel for the roads you walk,

she

she is relentless in her pursuit of the inspired path.

she has a box where she allows her fears to be acknowledged and stored. she is blind to limitations and audacious in her ability to inquire and ask for help.

Afraid of both ledges and heights, she climbs while looking up.

she accomplishes things because it doesn't occur to her that she can't. she is annoying in her persistence: she is persistent anyway.

she laughs unfettered in enclosed spaces and cries without apology when she is stirred. often she arrives where she didn't know she was headed. she recognizes home when she sees it.

she is determined.

I call myself determined. I like the sound of it. On the observing side, or the other end of my pursuits, I've been called tenacious, fierce, relentless. I know they are not intended much as a compliment—but that is how I take it. Often I just knock on different doors until one of them opens (or I find a hidden key!). Sometimes I go around, or climb in through a window. It's an irony of determination that I must also know when to step aside from the journey. When I am committed to something I know my determination, in step with my imagination, will find a road.

-Mary Anne Radmacher

People are like stained-glass windows. They sparkle and shine when the sun is out, but when the darkness sets in, their true beauty is revealed only if there is a light from within.

-ELISABETH KÜBLER-ROSS

The most effective way to do it is to do it.

-AMELIA EARHART

I see my body as an instrument, rather than an ornament.

-ALANIS MORISSETTE

Courage is fear that has said its prayers.

-DOROTHY BERNARD

True Champions aren't always the ones that win, but those with the most guts.

-MIA HAMM

Movement never lies. It is a barometer telling the state of the soul's weather.

-MARTHA GRAHAM

Nobody has ever measured, not even poets, how much the heart can hold.

-ZELDA FITZGERALD

It was to her faults that she turned to save herself now.

-MADELEINE L'ENGLE

Dear One Who is Strong in Spirit,

Your perseverance seems boundless. Just when it looks like you have been tangled in an impasse, that your feet are bound—Something Happens. It's as if you cast off the lines of all your obstacles and sail off—the wind of determination blowing in your sails. In fact, this poem reminds me a lot of you:

The Maybe's and the Should Have's and the
Could Have's and the Naught's
the Might Have Been's and Could Have Been's
can all be stuffed into a box.

If Only and Perhaps I Might
can join them all right there.
I'd add Probably and Ought To Have
for a wee bit of flashy flair.

And then I Will, I Must, I Shall
turn that box loose upon the water.
May it float straight to hell and
give those folks some fodder.

For the Doubt, the Wondering,
the Second Guessing—All—
create a grand disturbance in
the Peace—Just Like A Fall.

And once that box has been sent off
and the room and air are cleared,
I'll look square in the sparkly mirror,
"There's no doubt left, no fear."

Finished speaking, I turn around
for all the world to see
the courage and determination
that's been called from within me.

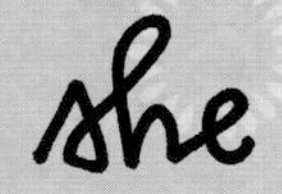

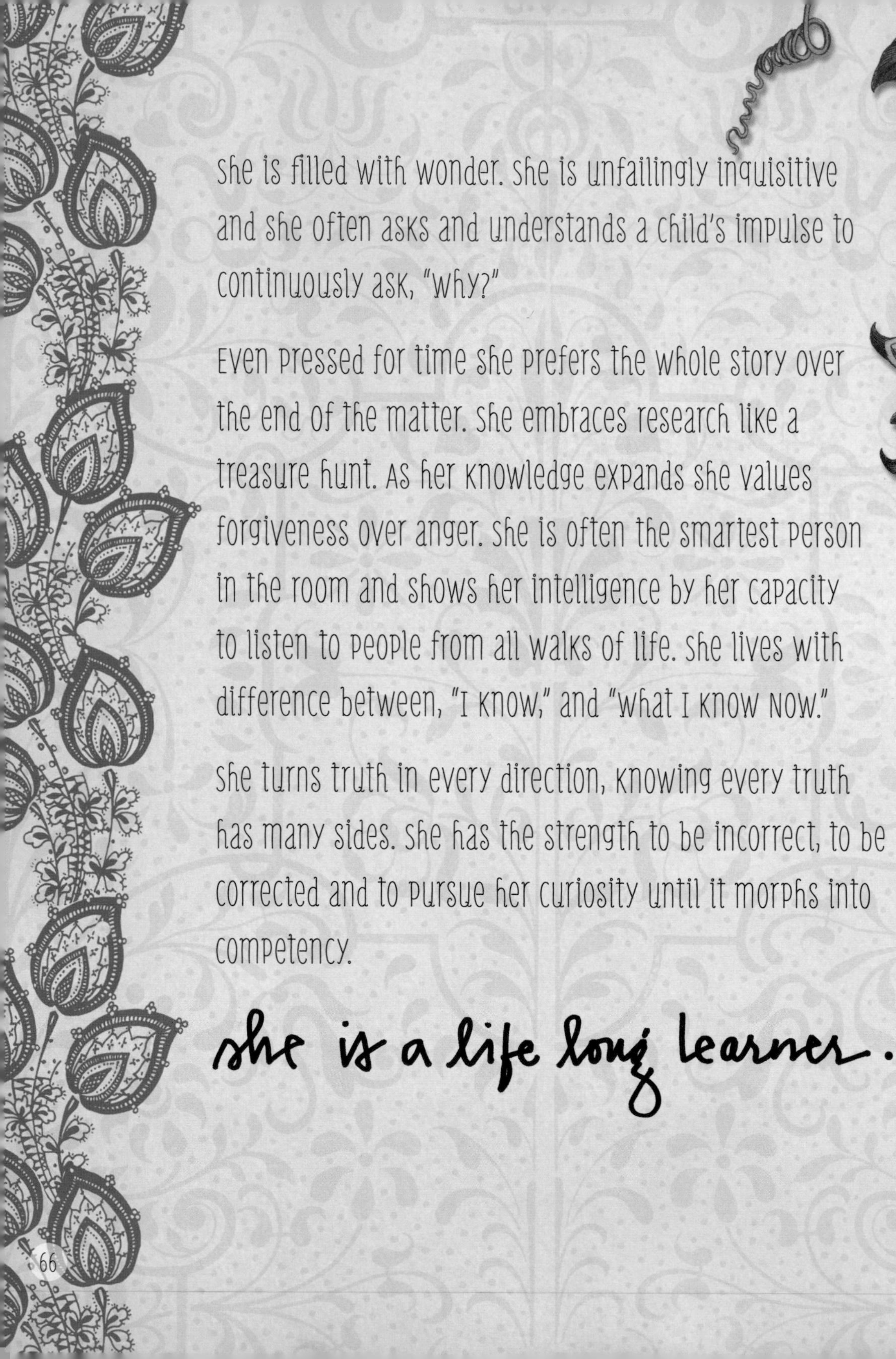

She is filled with wonder. She is unfailingly inquisitive and she often asks and understands a child's impulse to continuously ask, "why?"

Even pressed for time she prefers the whole story over the end of the matter. She embraces research like a treasure hunt. As her knowledge expands she values forgiveness over anger. She is often the smartest person in the room and shows her intelligence by her capacity to listen to people from all walks of life. She lives with difference between, "I know," and "what I know now."

She turns truth in every direction, knowing every truth has many sides. She has the strength to be incorrect, to be corrected and to pursue her curiosity until it morphs into competency.

she is a life long learner.

"Be curious earlier," a friend often reminds me. Maybe curiosity is the funniest way to happiness? Certainly, when we are curious, we are present—our whole being is captivated, listening, responding. When we are curious, we drop our judgments and preconceptions (at least a little). But, maybe best of all, being curious reminds us we can always, always evolve, adapt, soften and yes, change. That nothing—truly nothing—is fixed in this whole darn amazing universe. If I can be anything more often and earlier, it's curious. For then, I become a flexible prayer bending with what life brings. I embrace being an imperfect learner, taking new shapes every day, and leaving old stories behind. I am free to keep discovering just who I really am.

-Jennifer Louden

Perhaps the secret of living well is not in having all the answers but in pursuing unanswerable questions in good company.

-RACHEL NAOMI REMEN

We learn as much from sorrow as from joy, as much from illness as from health, from handicap as from advantage—and indeed perhaps more.

-PEARL S. BUCK

If you are interested, you never have to look for new interests, they come to you. When you are genuinely interested in one thing, it will always lead to something else.

-ELEANOR ROOSEVELT

The cure for boredom is curiosity. There is no cure for curiosity.

-DOROTHY PARKER

Learning is not attained by chance. It must be sought for with ardor and attended to with diligence.

-ABIGAIL ADAMS

I am learning all the time. The tombstone will be my diploma.

-EARTHA KITT

Do not call for black power or green power. Call for brain power.

-BARBARA JORDAN

I loved getting A's. I liked being smart. I liked being on time. I thought being smart is cooler than anything in the world.

-MICHELLE OBAMA

Greetings, Perennial Student—

Your curiosity can be maddening. I know there are times you wish those questions which run constantly would just still themselves. WHY? HOW? or the increasingly common, "Why not?" populate your hours. Even in your sleep inquiry asserts itself and you wake to the day with a hunger to know more. Such an inquisitive nature guarantees that boredom does not knock on your door. If there is a problem with a life long commitment to knowledge gathering, it is that there is an endless supply of stuff to know. The potential for feeling done, the satisfaction of being completed is elusive. For surely as one level of competency is acquired, it gives the view to how much more there is to see. Just because you knew something once doesn't mean it's still true. There's the other part—keeping up with shifts, changes, developments. Fortunately there's a core of truth that is not subject to upgrade...the love of a bird in flight, the appreciation of the light as morning opens to dawn. These things are immutable. What a relief!

One of the things I value most deeply about you is, in spite of the depth of your knowledge, you are at ease with wholeheartedly declaring, "I don't know." Then it's reasonably certain you will quickly set about discovering what new thing you can learn.

When I want to know...I know who to call,

she

She uncovers other ways and she discovers fresh voices.

She studies her own and the successes of others. She holds observation and learning as a starting place, not an ending.

She mixes ideas and strategies like a chemist mixes compounds. She constantly wonders and is inspired by awe.

Her friends hold on to the closest railing when she starts a sentence, "What if we...?"

She rests from all the things she dreams of exploring and creating when her soul is too full. She pours fascination in and pours out possibilities.

she is imaginative.

We are all creative souls with the power to make new connections in our thinking and create the new. As women, we intuitively innovate everyday in some aspect of our lives. Our imagination and ingenuity spark clever insights, solutions, and creations which become part of our life story. Let's encourage our sisters to weave their own inventions and share their inspiring tales as well. Own your gift of creative making and celebrate it! Nourish the joy of creation, whatever the "art" of your choosing, and allow yourself to feel the pleasure and the empowerment of your results.

-Gail McMeekin

When you take a flower in your hand and really look at it—it's your world for a moment.

-GEORGIA O'KEEFE

It is the ability to choose which makes us human.

-MADELEINE L'ENGLE

Sometimes things go wrong to teach you what is right.

-ALICE WALKER

We spent a lot of time wondering if we were "normal." Some of us decided we weren't. Ready to wear did not quite fit us.

-MARGARET ATWOOD

Success breeds confidence.

-BERYL MARKHAM

Resolve to take Fate by the throat and shake a living out of her.

-LOUISA MAY ALCOTT

The Possible's slow fuse is lit by the imagination.

-EMILY DICKINSON

Salutations to You, Inventive Sister—

Even though many of your creations are discoveries of your own, you are willing, at every turn, to answer the eager question, "How'd you do that?" Recipe keeping has never held any attraction for you. You encourage everyone to share what they know. You adhere to the principle that we are better and stronger when we work together. That's you—nourishing the joy in yourself and others.

You seem especially gifted with "I" words, which is ironic since you focus so little attention on the "I" of yourself. Imaginative. Inventive. Innovative. Intuitive. Instinctive. They all stew together in the cauldron of your empowering actions.

Your imagination has served you well. There have been plenty of tough spots—the imagination engine has pulled you out of all of them. Imagination is a cross discipline for you—it is put to work in every area of your life. I note that you've trained yourself to never say, "I can't imagine myself doing that." Instead, like trying a bright red sweater you say, "I'm going to see if I can imagine myself doing that." Rather than closing the door on any possibility, you open a window and say, "Let's just see what we can see."

Yes, you have the courage to look when you are on that big roller coaster when other people just squeeze their eyes tight and hold on.

I learn from you that the bigger you allow your imagination to be—the more surprising your results will be.

Daring to dream,

she offers kindness and lives with compassion. she knows that in answering one need she serves the world. she invests in herself and others. familiar with the word, no, she does not let fear or uncertainty keep her from asking.

she feels requesting help and offering help are both found along the same line. grateful for hands she has taken hold of in the course of her life makes a compelling case for extending the same kind support to others. she does not believe in an accidental encounter. she is inspired by generosity. she also knows how to receive with grace. she is amazing.

she is in service.

I rarely think of what I do in terms of it being service. But I recognize that people consider it that. For me, it's as simple as seeing a need, creating a solution and making it available. Maybe it's because I'm an artist that making a solution for a problem feels artful. Some of my closest friends say I operate with "zero degrees of separation" because I don't observe traditional barriers. If I see opportunity for "service" I'll either act on it myself or always reach out and ask. Yes. Always ask.

-Connie Fails

I felt it shelter to speak to you.

-EMILY DICKINSON

Where there is great love there are always miracles.

-WILLA CATHER

Never doubt that a small group of thoughtful, committed citizens can change the world. Indeed, it is this only thing that ever has.

-MARGARET MEAD

Education is for improving the lives of others and for leaving your community and world better than you found it.

-MARIAN WRIGHT EDELMAN

Politics has less to do with where you live than where your heart is.

-MARGARET CHO

When you cease to make a contribution you begin to die.

-ELEANOR ROOSEVELT

Those who don't know how to weep with their whole heart don't know how to laugh either.

-GOLDA MEIR

Service is the rent we pay for living.

-MARIAN WRIGHT EDELMAN

She Who Offers Solutions in Service:

You've had an eye for filling needs since you were little. It seems as normal to you as breathing. People love watching you make things happen—it's almost like watching magic. It looks so straightforward and easy when you do. And you often say that it is. You have been heard to say time and again that you aren't asking people to give up anything, you are giving them an opportunity to contribute to something that matters. Something that makes a difference.

I know you well enough to know that sometimes it's not as easy as it looks. Yet still you persevere. How many lives have been changed, improved or saved because you had the nerve to reach out, the courage to ask for the contribution or the commitment? I see you smile and say, "What's the worst thing that could happen, someone will say NO?"

When you are unable, personally, to provide a service or fill a need, I've seen you go out and find someone who can. In this process I marvel at your balance. You don't think you can save the world, just the part of the world that shows up in front of you. I've heard you say, "No thank you," to the opportunity of service. I learn from you that your *no* becomes the opportunity for someone else's *yes*. You have a sense of clarity about what is within your own skill set. And within that set, nothing seems impossible to you. Your sense of service is a clear, strong river and those who swim in the tide are forever changed.

With strong admiration,

she

She dances. She laughs. She sings. She paints. She creates. She can take an ordinary nothing and turn it into an extraordinary something.

She does not find, "never done it before, " a legitimate reason to not make, or create something. "Never before," translates in her language to, "just haven't tried it yet." It is not accurate to say she is fearless. She entertains her share of fears. She is constant in her certainty of creation. She is persistent in her passion for discovering beauty.

She knows how to turn frowns upside down—she makes every good thing even better.

she is creative.

To be creative, is to be human, it's really that simple. Creativity is an integral part of our humanity, our existence and our experience on this earth. Sometimes we wait: wait for the right moment, wait for just the right set of tools, the right skill set or the right medium. I want to say to you: don't wait. Start right where you are, right in this moment. Dive into the stories you want to tell, the experiences you are longing to share, the knowledge you have gained, the images that are an expression of your soul. Create because you can. Create because the act of creating will remind you of who you truly are. Create because it brings you joy, and peace, and vitality. Create because the rest of us need to hear your voice, added to the chorus.

-Liz Kalloch

It is the function of art to renew our perception.

-ANAÏS NIN

A child's attitude toward everything is an artist's attitude.

-WILLA CATHER

The most potent tool for contacting inner guidance and creativity is walking.

-JULIA CAMERON

Creativity comes from trust. Trust your instincts. And never hope more than you work.

-RITA MAE BROWN

Dancing: The highest intelligence in the freest body.

-ISADORA DUNCAN

Ah, music...a magic beyond all we do here!

-J. K. ROWLING

It had never occurred to me before that music and thinking are so much alike. In fact you could say music is another way of thinking, or maybe thinking is another kind of music.

-URSULA LE GUIN

I believe that true identity is found... in creative activity springing from within. It is found, paradoxically, when one loses oneself.

-ANNE MORROW LINDBERGH

All artists dream of a silence they must enter, as some creatures return to the sea to spawn.

-IRIS MURDOCH

I cultivate being uppity. It's something my gramom taught me.

-KATE RUSHIN

Hello to the Original Thinker!

Your creative process appears every bit like a simmering, sensational pot of yumminess. Stew comes to mind but that's too ordinary. You keep dozens of delicious "pots" of juicy amazingness simmering on low, all the time! You are so connected to the right time for each of these things. It's remarkable, really, that you have such a capacity. It's like what they say about Jello, there's always room.

I know, for a fact, that you periodically experience uncertainty about a thing you are making, inventing, building. I know because you tell me. Occasionally you encounter fear on the way to something new. You sometimes wonder about timing because you've had the experience of being both ahead of the curve and a little behind the trend. In either event, you seem to come to the same conclusion, what matters most is if you like it. If it is the right time and the right thing for you—then all the external stuff, and the wondering about it all, seems to fade into its proper place in perspective.

Your creative capacity speaks many different languages. You can create as a mirror for another or you give voice and form to ideas and things that are unique and so utterly you. In any event, you are thoughtful about the beauty or whimsey you are bringing to the world. It's as if you are inviting dear, personal friends out to a grand dance. And, in a way, you are.

Your creativity softens the edges of a harsh world. More importantly it softens the edges of your world. In those blissful moments of making, when there is no fear, no wondering, you remember why it is you do this thing. It brightens a day, connects a friend to a friend. Not only is your work good work, but it does good work in the world.

Oh, please, make something!

PS: Do you need to be reminded that your friends have among their "favorite things" items that you have created just for them? They do. Be reminded.

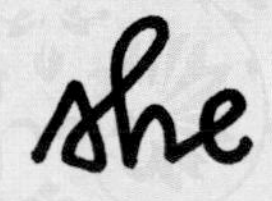

she is ready to greet you where she is—and where you are. she practices a hospitality that transcends the walk to her open door. she opens her heart, with confidence and vulnerability, and invites a gentle walk within. she knows when to pull her shades and hang a sign that reads, "not now, perhaps soon."

she's far more inclined to fuss over the wrapping of a gift than she is over dust on a mantle. she appreciates a well ordered home but values a well-tended friend even more. sparkling conversation has priority over cleaning dishes after dinner.

A guest feels the sense of a hearty, "HELLO! It's you!" whether that enthusiasm comes from opening her door or opening a piece of mail. Her cup of tea soothes and satisfies long after the cup is emptied.

In filling up others, she herself is filled.

she is welcoming.

wel·come [wel-kuh m] interjection, noun, verb, wel·comed, wel·com·ing, adjective. interjection 1. (a word of kindly greeting, as to one whose arrival gives pleasure): Welcome, stranger! noun 2. a kindly greeting or reception, as to one whose arrival gives pleasure: to give someone a warm welcome.

verb (used with object) 3. to greet the arrival of (a person, guests, etc.) with pleasure or kindly courtesy. 4. to receive or accept with pleasure; regard as pleasant or good: to welcome a change. 5. to meet, accept, or receive (an action, challenge, person, etc.) in a specified, especially unfriendly, manner: They welcomed him with hisses and catcalls.

All we want, really, is to be warm, safe, appreciated and loved. It is just that simple, and it doesn't need to be fancy. Warm blankets, soft pillows, good coffee, and a sturdy table around which conversation, laughter and joy can be shared are all that's needed. When our hearts are open, and we are present in all the moments we share with others, we can't help but feel welcome with one another, and receive what our hearts need most.

-Christine Mason Miller

It is not how much we do, but how much love we put in the doing. It is not how much we give, but how much love is put in the giving.

-MOTHER TERESA

Sometimes you can't see yourself clearly until you see yourself through the eyes of others.

-ELLEN DEGENERES

Being a good listener is not the same as not talking.

-MARGARET ATWOOD

The real art of conversation is not only to say the right thing in the right place, but to leave unsaid the wrong thing at the tempting moment.

-LADY DOROTHY NEVILL

At the worst, a house unkempt cannot be so distressing as a life unlived.

-ROSE MACAULAY

You grow up the day that you have your first real laugh at yourself.

-ETHEL BARRYMORE

Home is a gift to be opened every day.

-MARY ANNE RADMACHER

She is always optimistic and resourceful, a woman who, if cast ashore alone on a desert island, would build a house with a guest room.

-EDNA BUCHANAN

She Who Offers a Warm Welcome—

Your hospitable embrace is felt whether it is radiating from a surprise package that just arrived at my door or if it is you opening the door to your home. You have an extraordinary capacity to make visitors feel like family and that it would be impossible to overstay the welcome. It's sort of ironic that people comment they feel more "at home" with you in your home than they feel in their own. How do you do that?

You've told your friends that there used to be a time that you worried about how your house looked and if there was dust in the corners. That time has passed. I must say I've yet to notice any dust in any of your corners, but perhaps that is because when visiting with you there are so many marvelous distractions. Extraordinary food that is beautiful, healthy and delicious (did I already say HOW do you do that?), engaging conversation, wildly rewarding activities. Actually sometimes visiting you feels a bit like being on retreat and a little like being at summer camp. All in one remarkable experience.

I learn a lot about welcoming people to my own home by being welcomed into yours. Instead of feeling intimidated by how easy you make things look—I ask myself to think about how YOU would prepare for anticipated guests and then I pretend it is easy. And, most of the time it is. I know that the welcoming is the quality of attentiveness...not if the kitchen is sparkling or how impressive the food I offer is (although I must say, I notice your kitchen sparkles and the spread is always impressive!). I have learned that little things matter. In fact, one might say that the little things turn out to be the big things. The sweet things you leave out for your guests, the welcome note, the time that you sent a note thanking me for being your guest. Surprise and delight. That's it—two of the most essential ingredients that are part of being welcomed by you.

Grateful to know I've a home away from home,

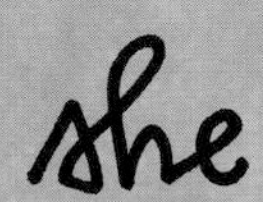

she seeks beauty in all things. she creates and gathers environments, tools and things that support her keenly honed sense of calling.

she recognizes objects have more value because of their meaning than their making. she restores order in the midst of chaos by breathing in the aspirations of her soul and breathing out the intentions behind what she makes.

uncommon enterprises touch her, she cries at the great events of the world expressed in a spectrum from profound loss to stunning triumph. the ornament of her thinking is well-composed and is lovely to consider.

she owns the right kind of boots for walking through mud. she welcomes birth in all its uncomfortable and amazing forms. she seasons her days with the spice of luscious mystery.

she is an exquisite aesthetic.

Being an Exquisite Aesthetic is a way of rising gently with each breath. It is not a superficial luxury in this world; it is an urgent necessity. It is being a light in the darkness, a protest against ugliness, a harmonic in dissonance, order in the midst of chaos. It is a political statement. It is a spiritual practice. It is a cause, and it is a calling. It is a line in the sand, a sign of determined resolution that proclaims that no matter what appearances or predictions might say, the Sacred does surround us. We are enfolded in the Holy. There is always something lovely to be found, always; and the search for it or deliberate creation of it is never frivolous. John Keats was right: Beauty is Truth, Truth Beauty.

-Maggie Oman Shannon

The moment of change is the only poem.

-ADRIENNE RICH

Our truest response to the irrationality of the world is to paint or sing or write, for only in such response do we find truth.

-MADELEINE L'ENGLE

Beauty is not caused. It is.

-EMILY DICKINSON

You were given life; it is your duty (and also your entitlement as a human being) to find something beautiful within life, no matter how slight.

-ELIZABETH GILBERT

But he who dares not grasp the thorn should never crave the rose.

-ANNE BRONTË

Beauty is how you feel inside, and it reflects in your eyes. It is not something physical.

-SOPHIA LOREN

I want to see beauty. In the ugly, in the sink, in the suffering, in the daily, in all the days before I die, the moments before I sleep.

-ANN VOSKAMP

Think of all the beauty still left around you and be happy.

-ANNE FRANK

Salutations to SHE who finds beauty in unlikely places...

You do indeed have an exquisite aesthetic. The spaces and places you create around yourself are less composed than they are orchestrated. You have a lovely way of combining objects that are meaningful to you...in a way that touches others.

The items that surround you are as diverse as you are. And some of them are so ordinary it's curious that you can make them appear so special. A rock. A stone. A feather. You've said they are sacred and that is how they present themselves. A stone from a beach, a rock from a path, and a priceless object of art. All together. Creating a canvas that is a visual representation of your life.

There is a certain timelessness about you. Some consider you trendy and yet your choices transcend what is current or popular. Much of what is in your line of sight is there because it has a story, is iconic, represents an important person or lesson. And the impact of that is so much deeper than what is currently fashionable.

Your friends are reminded that a thing needn't be "art" in order to be artful. And that is demonstrated by you every day—not only in what surrounds you but by what is extended to the world from within you.

Appreciating beauty in more places because of you,

she

she sees and hears. she listens to herself and others. she naps with power and speed. she's at ease with rulers or riff-raff.

she is quick to offer easy grace to those who choose vastly different ways from hers. she requires, however, reciprocal grace, in that she is unwilling to allow others to impose their ways or roads upon her. on this point she is pointedly clear. she is often heard to respond to harshness or inventive drama or conflict with a rather stand-offish, "well, there you are." And there the drama will stay because her pervasive peace of mind wants none of it.

when giving directions she is more inclined to describe, "a way to go," rather than, "the only route to take..." And this is how she maintains the equanimity in her days. she embraces the truth of the moment as her truth, in this moment. changes blow in with every wind and with an easy sigh she can say good-by to what was and sit, welcoming the moment that is. children and dogs like her especially well. she has an easy and engaging way of being in the world.

she is contentment.

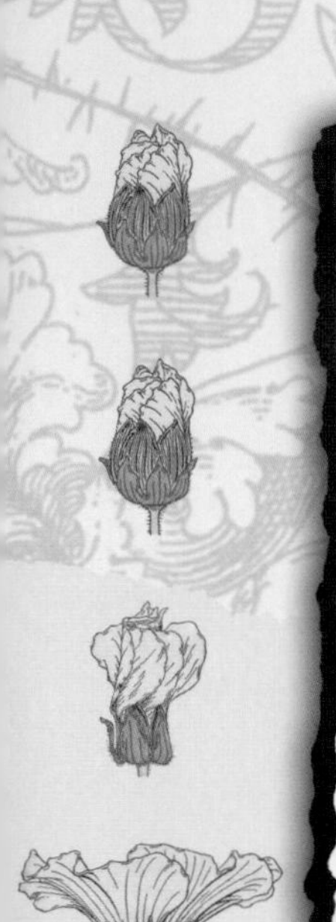

Full circle, caring, giving, receiving,
timeless accepting, true blue, real deal,
no perfection here,
planting heart seeds daily,
harnessing the power of LOVE,
striving always to be a SHE who is authentically ME,
a strong,
lucky,
playful,
generous,
kind journeyer.

-Caren Albers

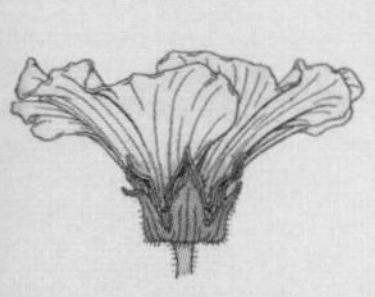

Being present requires profound concentration on what we're doing as we go along.

-ALEXANDRA STODDARD

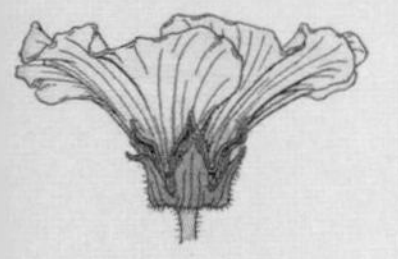

There must be quite a few things a hot bath won't cure, but I don't know many of them.

-SYLVIA PLATH

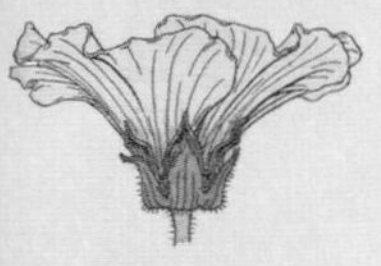

What people think of me is none of my business.

-TERRY COLE WHITTAKER

Our visions begin with our desires.

-AUDRE LORDE

The people and circumstances around me do not make me what I am, they reveal who I am.

-LAURA SCHLESSINGER

There are no little things. "Little things," so called, are the hinges of the universe.

-FANNY FERN

To be really great in little things, to be truly noble and heroic in the insipid details of everyday life is a virtue so rare as to be worthy of canonization.

-HARRIET BEECHER STOWE

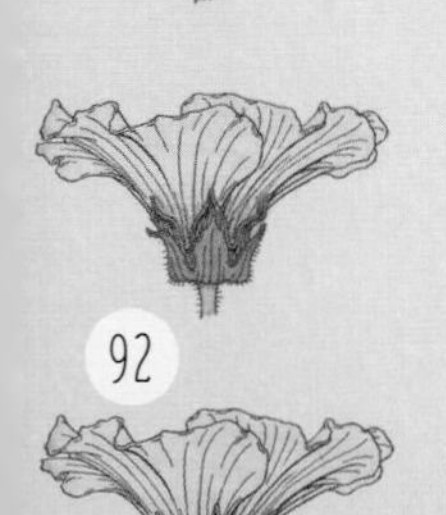

Dear One—

It is appropriate to rest. It is acceptable to “do nothing.” And, actually, that’s a misnomer. Doing “nothing” is doing something. Something very important for your level of ease and your sense of well being. It is tempting with all that is on “the list” to create pressure for yourself. Achieve. Do. Reach for excellence. More and more after that. All those are fabulous invitations, particularly if the doing is a lovely match for your passions and sense of calling. Knowing to insert health, wellness and personal joys into “the list” is essential.

The press of “doing” is often sweeping at your heels, driving you into doing just one more thing. A holiday experience doesn’t have to translate into days or weeks away. You can strike a five minute yoga pose, you can take a 15 minute walk, have a 30 minute conversation with a faraway friend. You can sit and absorb the beauty that surrounds you in your own home or yard. There will always be plenty of busy-ness awaiting you on the other side of your door marked, “Contentment.” Make the next thing on your list an endeavor that restores you and infuses you with the perspective of ease and satisfaction. The capacity to rest and restore is a companion of contentment and a hallmark of deep personal confidence. Being busy constantly is not what makes you—you. Being utterly comfortable with the core of who you are—now there’s YOU looking in the mirror! Please, go ahead. Put your feet up and enjoy the wonder as you consider the blessings of your world.

Much love.

she

she is an expert at practicing the pause. she knows that patience is more than a virtue, it's a key to her grace. she is poised and at ease.

she uses two mantras often, "don't take it personally, it's rarely about you," and "my job? my responsibility. not my job? not my story." when she forgets—she stands in front of the mirror and remembers herself back to her core.

she resists good intentions all showing up at once as well as poor choices knocking, one bad habit at a time. she practices the benefit of the purposeful pauses.

she recognizes that choosing to take no action at all is still quite something. she holds her own truth while honoring the knowing of others. she lives with intention.

she is a model of balance.

My idea of "balance" changes from day to day. What's true and balanced on one day may need to change in a different circumstance. Balance requires continual assessment. I strive to recognize the opportunity for pauses in my life and embrace patience. It's been a progressive process. One of the most important phrases in my balancing act is, "No, thank you."

-Kim Hamilton

"A life of obvious and clear balance may be overrated. The balance that works in real life is the pace that radiates from a person's core and maintains an inner equilibrium in the midst of the messy, wild ride which is the road of everyday life."

-MARY ANNE RADMACHER

It is in our idleness, in our dreams, that the submerged truth sometimes comes to the top.

-VIRGINIA WOOLF

Once life slows down enough for reflection, women uncover truths several beats away from the expected and the promised.

-MARJORIE ANDERSON

I love myself when I am laughing, and then again when I am looking mean and impressive.

-ZORA NEALE HURSTON

Power is the ability not to have to please.

-ELIZABETH JANEWAY

I restore myself when I am alone. A career is born in public—talent in privacy.

-MARILYN MONROE

Hello to She Who Harnesses Her Harmony,

Your balancing act has changed over the years. It used to remind me of that professional juggler who could spin dinner plates on broom handles and not drop any of them. These days your balance seems less about spinning plates and more about focus.

One of the things I've learned from you is not to allow myself to be governed by the tyranny of others' immediacy. What might be a crisis to someone else truly has to stand in line at your door. They can't just expect to always bully themselves to the front of the line by declaring a state of emergency. I just realized, you've balanced those "bullies" right out of your immediate life experience. And you did it in such a gentle way I hardly noticed until now. This makes me smile—you even have a balanced approach to the way you dispense your balance.

One of the graces of athletes with balance is that it appears effortless. Yet it is clear there is years of effort and commitment behind that appearance. You have also done your work. And you continue to do that "work" each and every day. I know you have practices, you exercise, you do your own spiritual practice, you connect to the glories in nature. I've also observed you practicing a form of hibernation...a kind "not now, but soon," sign posted on the door of your days. Everything does indeed get its due season...in the right time.

I have learned that there need be no apology for choosing your needs first above the needs of others. In fact, making that choice is what brings that sense of ease and proportion into your days. It might have been true for Mae West that "too much of a good thing can be wonderful," yet in the recipe that is your life, too much of one thing spoils the whole thing. All things in their correct measure is a marvelous motto. And it is that measure that allows you to take notice when things are having an agreeable equilibrium.

With an appreciative and encouraged sigh,

she

she helps. she holds. she's fierce as she raises up her friend. she's steadfast and supportive. she says, "I'll stay. don't worry." she walks before to guide, behind to protect and beside to uplift and she laughs.

she expands with joys shared. she lifts up, packs in, moves forward and leaves sorrows behind. she talks as well as she listens. she celebrates successes and sympathizes with less than stellar experiences.

Even when she can't say, "I know," she says, "I can imagine." she shows up—at just the right time. every delight in life is made sweeter and each burden lightened when shared with a friend.

she is a fine, kind friend.

I am blessed with many friends and a few of them for now over 50 years. We have ridden out storms, celebrated anything that calls for celebration and stood by one another through the peaks, valley, pits and chasms of life.

THE KEY:

(1) Absolute love and adoration, including our blemishes and shortcomings.

(2) Hold them close with the highest esteem.

(3) Don't ever, even when life gets really busy, take the richness of the friendship for granted.

-Barbara Joy

Open your heart, fling your hopes high, set your dreams aloft. I am here to hold your hand.

-MAYA ANGELOU

Friendship with oneself is all important beccause without it one cannot be friends with anyone else in the world.

-ELEANOR ROOSEVELT

The hearts that never lean, must fall.

-EMILY DICKINSON

Each person's life is lived as a series of conversations.

-DEBORAH TANNEN

My means of empowerment has always been to search out wonderful friends—people who believe in me, who help me believe in myself.

-SANDY WARSHAW

Constant use had not worn ragged the fabric of their friendship.

-DOROTHY PARKER

You are the time-worn pages of my favorite book.

-MARY ANNE RADMACHER

Friendship is the bread of the heart.

-MARY RUSSELL MITFORD

Dearest Friend,

You stand up for me. You sit down with me. You sing when I want to dance and you start twirling the baton when I am on the march. And when you are ready to lead the parade I'm the one in the back row. Yep, the one playing the tuba.

I'm winter to your autumn and you are summer to my spring. I like that we are different. Our differences make us stronger. And give us awesome stories to share. I think we are different enough that we surprise some folks that we are friends. But once they hear us laughing together, there's no longer any surprise. And when I don't get the joke, you whisper the point of the punchline in my ear. And you assure me that it's charming that I laugh longer than anyone else—even though we both know it's because I'm last to get the joke.

We have weathered some hard seasons and we have watched each other let some friendships go. Ours remains strong for many reasons that I know, and some for reasons of mystery that is beyond us both. When you could have judged me, you accepted my best of the moment. When you could have said, "How many times do I have to tell you?" you just found a fresh way to say the same truth. You help me remember the best parts of myself and you find the best parts when I've misplaced them. You show me the best way to be a friend by the careful tending you extend to yourself.

In knowing you I have discovered that I'm the truest friend I can be to me, before I can be a fine friend for someone else. Even when we don't talk, I can hear you. And even when we're far apart, the distance cannot matter between us for ours is a friendship of the heart.

Friends, always.

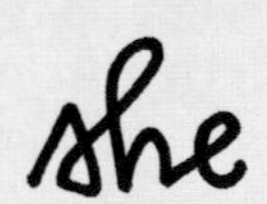

There is a world of wisdom in the collective knowing of your wise friends. To demonstrate I asked a broad circle of my friends to share how they encourage and uplift themselves. The result is a wonderful loving letter from SHE's all over.

Dear Sweet SHE,

Remember to be grateful. Moving and dancing helps change a mood. Anxiety has a beginning, middle and end...it will pass. Just ride the wave. Trust the flow—it's easier to move with the river than fight it. When you panic remembering a moment and wishing you had acted differently—remind yourself that is now history. I remind myself of the times I have overcome my fears and that helps me remember that I can. Embrace the discomfort and learn from it—remembering the only time that ever really matters is now.

Surround yourself with colors and images that you like and, of course, wise words. When facing grief look for the loss to feel different, not "better." Remind yourself of all the difficult situations you have tackled and survived and that this is just one more chance to come out on the other side of "hard." Use other people's wisdom to begin tapping into your own. When you are in a black hole, depressed, it takes more than somebody saying, "Get out of there," to get out. There will be times when it is hard to dream. If you live your dreams long enough they will become your reality. You are enough: you are. Love, be loved. Look at your family and let your love for them call you back to yourself. You are whatever you choose to be, you are wherever you want to be and your dreams have no limitations. Everybody gets stuck, sometimes, just in the process of surviving stuff...just do the next thing. One small step toward your dream pulls you a bit out of that stuck place.

Post quotes in your sightline that remind you of the need for community, belonging and connection. Even if it's hard to work through the fear or to set the fear to the side, we always have the control over how we feel about a thing. You get to determine how life goes by choosing the way you look at it and how you react to things. Our senses can guide us to the place we want to be—we just need to choose a thing that will help make a shift—music, smell, taste. We are not alone. Anxious moments will arise so own them, name them and redirect them by making a different choice. Coming down hard on the flaws of others is really coming down hard on your own flaws: speak only good about others. Surround yourself with universal true statements that lift your attitude. When you change the way you look at things, the things you look at change. Remember encouraging things like, "Courage doesn't always roar. Sometimes courage is the quiet voice at the end of the day saying, 'I will try again tomorrow.'" Be right here, right now. Every day you wake up, each moment, is a gift. Don't take it for granted. Remember to breathe.

With Love from,

Suzanne Landers Stevens; Courtney Putnam; Theresa Shreffler; Susan Rubes; Melissa Hudspeth McCurdy; Cyndy Smith Dalton; Kelly Bennett; Karen Ferguson Johnson; Ellen Lambert Cunningham; Marion Cepican; Lisa Vetter; Kathie Care; Mimi Glavin; Odie Pahl; Cathy Culver Koch; Michelle Fairchild; Monica Kitchens Schruhl; Charla Kinzel; Lynne Bergman; Shelly Johnson Miller; Carol Reshenk Minor; Susan Opeka; Victoria Perkins; Linda T. Marsh; Roxanne Teuscher Custer

In our finest world stand loving men who are witness to our capacity to harness everything.

Here are some messages for you from a few of them:

Dear Divine SHE,

SHE is both creator and inspiration for my creativity. Her perspective turns my solo view into 3-D; and her varied colors enliven my monotones. I do so love HER.

Divorce doubt and get engaged with confidence. Embrace music that lifts you high and inspires you to be unafraid to be...you. "Build a bridge—and get over it," is a great expression, however, every person and every situation is different. Only you'll know when you've reached the other side. I am not a victim. No matter what I have been through, I'm still here. I have a history of victory.

Contributors: David Kinne; Chris Bartlett; Jay Jellinek; Steve Maraboli

About our Contributors and Role Models

CONTRIBUTORS

CAREN ALBERS is a blogger and writing coach. Her commitment to contentment and creating impacts all her actions—including her role as a grandmother. carenalbersinspirations.com, carenalbers.blogspot.com, skirt.com

GINA BRAMUCCI continues her human rights work and her travels. She lives with her family in France. flickr.com/photos/temoignages

DEANNA DAVIS, Ph.D., is an author, consultant, speaker, coach, publisher, and comedian. deannadavis.net, appliedinsight.net

PATTI DIGH is a writer, speaker, and teacher who focuses on five core questions: Have I loved well? Have I lived fully? Have I let go deeply? Have I made a difference? and What would I be doing today if I only had 37 days to live? 37days.com

MARIANNE ELLIOTT is the author of *Zen Under Fire: Finding Peace in the Midst of War*, the story of her experience as a human rights monitor in Afghanistan. She is the creator of the online programs 30 Days of Yoga and 30 Days of Courage. A former UN peacekeeper and human rights lawyer, and currently a storyteller and yoga teacher, Marianne is the leader of Off the Mat, Into the World in New Zealand and Australia. marianne-elliott.com.

CONNIE FAILS and her designs are part of international fashion collections and have been featured in the *New York Times, Washington Post, USA Today, Vanity Fair, People,* and on *The Today Show* and *Good Morning America*. She supports service organizations worldwide, has acted as a White House Delegate of the Private Sector on the International Treaty on Adoption in The Hague and Netherlands. Fails manages the Clinton Museum Store for the Clinton Foundation in Little Rock, Arkansas. She is relentlessly innovative in all her activities and if it will fit on her machine she will sew on anything. conniefails.com

KATHLEEN GALLAGHER EVERETT is an author, nurse and part-time fairy.

KIM HAMILTON is a licensed birth worker and internationally recognized designer.mudlark.com, healthynests.blogspot.com

BARBARA JOY is an author and coach. Her book titles, *Easy Does It, Mom* and *Moms to Moms*, capture her passion to support and honor the role of parenting. She is a speaker and offers family coaching in person and by phone. parentingwithjoy.com

LIZ KALLOCH is a creator of artful constructions. She helps others present their work to the world through her graphic design, and offers beauty from her own original art in many different forms. lizkallochdesigns.com

JEN LEE is a storyteller whose books, apparel, audio programs, courses and film aim to nourish and inspire. jenlee.net

JENNIFER LOUDEN writes books on well-being and personal wisdom, teaches and coaches. In her commitment to both savor and serve in her life, she makes time for whimsy and memorable moments. jenniferlouden.com

SHILOH SOPHIA MCCLOUD is an artist, teacher and poet who lives her life as a great adventure. She publishes books on creativity, teaches painting and writing online at Cosmic Cowgirls University and The Red Madonna, and has championed women's art. Her vision is a world where the image of the feminine is cherished and celebrated and where all beings are free to express their deepest soul songs. shilohsophia.com

GAIL MCMEEKIN is known as the Passionate Mentor/ Coach for Creative Women and is the author of *The 12 Secrets of Highly Creative Women* and *The 12 Secrets of Highly Successful Women* and encourages women to access their creative seeds and use it to harvest the gold in their hearts and their businesses. creativesuccess.com

CHRISTINE MASON MILLER is a writer and artist who has been creating, writing and exploring ever since she was a little girl. Her mission to inspire provides the foundation for all of her creative work; the desire to encourage others to pursue their passions and create a meaningful life is the common thread throughout an expansive body of work that includes mixed media collages, commercial illustration, photography, writing, teaching and speaking. christinemasonmiller.com

AMANDA OAKS is a professional kindness warrior. kindovermatter.com, hooptacular.com

MARY ANNE RADMACHER is called author, artist, actionista and trainer. She intentionally applies her passion for words and love of creativity to all her endeavors. Her work on posters, cards and licensed products finds its way around the world. maryanneradmacher.net

GLENIS REDMOND is a poet and teacher. glenisredmond.com, glenisredmond.tumblr.com, twitter.com/poetica11

MELODY ROSS is a barefoot artist, author and advocate (with wishes for living in a tree house behind her ranch in Idaho). She is a licensed product designer and founder of Brave Girls Club, where she combines her art making with her love for helping women light their own way back home. Melody helps women out of human trafficking to heal through art and journaling. She loves to find beauty in all things. She is a mother of five, and wife of her high school sweetheart. They comprise the beloved family who host quarterly art retreats at their ranch. melodyross.com, bravegirlsclub.com

Rev. MAGGIE OMAN SHANNON, M.A., through her books, magazine articles, workshops, retreats and blog, offers creative tools, resources and guidance for walking the modern contemplative path. maggieomanshannon.com

GILLIAN SIMON is the designer and CEO of Quotable Cards. quotablecards.com

MAYA STEIN is a ninja poet, writing guide and creative adventuress. She believes that much of writing is actually about seeing, about paying attention, listening in and getting up close and personal with the details. She has built a life practice based on this. mayastein.com

ROLE MODELS

MADELEINE ALBRIGHT: to learn more about Madeleine Albright, visit secretary.state.gov/www/albright/albright.html

HILLARY RODHAM CLINTON: to learn more about Hillary Rodham Clinton, visit whitehouse.gov/about/first-ladies/hillaryclinton

ABOUT JANE KIRKPATRICK

After spending a quarter century on a remote Oregon ranch on Starvation Lane, JANE KIRKPATRICK moved with her husband of 37 years to Central Oregon. She is currently working on her 27th book and 24th novel; most of her work is based on the lives of actual historical women. Her titles have been *New York Times* bestsellers, WILLA Literary Award winners, and finalists for Christy Awards, Oregon Book Awards and Inspirational Readers Choice Awards. In her previous life, she worked as a mental health consultant to the Warm Springs Indian Reservation and served as the director of a community mental health program. A Wisconsin native, Jane is a frequent retreat and program speaker across the United States, Europe, and Canada, celebrating the power of stories in our lives. Two dogs keep her company. Her latest novel is *One Glorious Ambition* from WaterBrook/Random House.

INDEX

About the Authors

MARY ANNE RADMACHER's words find their way around the world in homes, school rooms, board rooms, prison cells, offices and business centers and medical facilities. Her words are quoted on television, in other books, in eulogies, on wedding and church programs and in commencement speeches. She is listed in the *Oxford Dictionary of American Quotations.* She is the author of eleven books and the artist and author of hundreds of products. She lives with her husband and three dogs on Whidbey Island in Washington State. Her media compass point is maryanneradmacher.net.

LIZ KALLOCH is a designer, illustrator, painter, teacher and writer who lives in a turquoise house in San Rafael near the San Francisco Bay. Her work has taken her around the world, where she's designed for a diverse lot of industries: ceramics studios, gift publishers, book publishers, jewelry, newspapers, indie start-ups and a non-profit research institute. Her illustrations have graced some lovely books and publications and she dreams of having more time to invent some hand-drawn fonts. Liz's art and writing are featured in the book *Desire to Inspire: Using Creative Passion to Transform the World* and she is also featured in a documentary on working as an independent artist, called *Indie Kindred.* She sells her artwork and jewelry designs at etsy.com/shop/LizKalloch and you can find more of her art and writing at lizkallochdesigns.com.

To Our Readers

From the Authors

SHE honors and celebrates the greatness within every woman. This encompasses our gentleman readers—by calling it the "Divine Feminine" within!

We both celebrate women who embody qualities that are important to us. These women, by virtue of how they live out their days, become a guidepost for our own practices and habits.

Our lives are enhanced by the presence of dynamic and inspiring role models. A role model keeps us from reinventing every process in our lives. They are our waymakers and pathfinders. They provide patterns of ease, service, and empowerment. We long for this book to inspire you. We hope it will prompt you to create your own list of role models and discover how they can contribute to the quality of your life.

We stand up taller when we draw attention to the greatness and strengths within us and within the circle of our friends and our greater tribe. It's tempting to focus on deficits and the way that things have gone wrong. *SHE* is a beautiful demonstration of how powerful it is to focus on our strengths and on what has gone right! Choosing to praise and respect the greatness in our circle is an invitation for us to shine with distinction.

We're grateful you've embraced *SHE* and thank you as you consider sharing it with people who matter to you.

Liz Kalloch and Mary Anne Radmacher, Collaborative Shes

From the Publisher

Viva Editions publishes books that inform, enlighten, and entertain. We do our best to bring you, the reader, quality books that celebrate life, inspire the mind, revive the spirit, and enhance lives all around. Our authors are practical visionaries: people who offer deep wisdom in a hopeful and helpful manner. Viva was launched with an attitude of growth and we want to spread our joy and offer our support and advice where we can to help you live the Viva way: vivaciously!

We're grateful for all our readers and want to keep bringing you books for inspired living. We invite you to write to us with your comments and suggestions, and what you'd like to see more of. You can also sign up for our online newsletter to learn about new titles, author events, and special offers.

Viva Editions
2246 Sixth St.
Berkeley, CA 94710
www.vivaeditions.com
(800) 780-2279
Follow us on Twitter @vivaeditions
Friend/fan us on Facebook